Acclaim for Meera Nair's

VIDEO

"Captivating. . . . A gifted writer with a flair for storytelling, Nair creates passionate, distinctive characters, establishing herself as a writer to watch. . . . [She] infuses each tale with incisive details about Indian culture, from the magical to the mundane." —*USA Today*

"Powerful. . . . Emotionally nuanced. . . . Flawlessly executed. . . . Taken together, [these stories] span a wide swath of Indian experience. . . . [An] accomplished collection." —*Vogue*

"These stories are stunning: sensuous and touching and beautifully crafted. Deeply varied, and full of human understanding, they not only give us the sound and feel of South Asia today (without ever resorting to exoticism); they also suggest, subtly and movingly, how easily longing can be awakened, as the world begins to shift around us. I've never met Meera Nair, but I feel I'll be listening to her for a very long time to come." —Pico Iyer

"Memorable and moving. . . . Poignant. . . . Nair captures the voices of her countrymen to mesmerizing effect. . . . Like her predecessors, Arundhati Roy, Salman Rushdie, Vikram Seth and Bharati Mukherjee, Nair is adept at weaving tales that intertwine the choices of individuals with the intricacies of Indian culture. . . . [Her] transcendent prose and lack of didacticism will have readers waiting anxiously for a sequel." —*The Oregonian*

"Engaging. . . . With brushes both broad and fine, Nair paints a clear picture of a culture very different from our own."
—*The Providence Journal*

"A strong sense of character and place, and an impressive variety of themes and tones, distinguish this striking debut collection. . . . Comparable to Jhumpa Lahiri's Pulitzer winner *Interpreter of Maladies,* and very probably the beginning of a fine career."
—*Kirkus Reviews*

"Many readers may finish *Video* hoping someday to have numerous Meera Nair books to organize alphabetically, though even then their hands may stray to 'V' and the delight that began it all. . . . Her stories are so inventive that they make many of her predecessors' fictions look like sociological studies. . . . *Video* [presents] a whole world, with all its richness and variety."
—*The Washington Post*

"Indelible. . . . A quietly defiant work of gentle emotion."
—*The Austin Chronicle*

"Masterful. . . . Unflinching. . . . Abound[ing] with authenticity. . . . [Nair] deftly brings to life the array of peoples, cultures, social cleavages, and religions that live in a jumbled mix of tradition, modernity, and East-West confluences."
—*The Washington Times*

Meera Nair

VIDEO

Meera Nair was born and raised in India and came to
the United States in 1997 to study creative writing.
She received an M.A. from Temple University and an
M.F.A. from New York University, where she was a
New York Times fellow. Her stories have been pub-
lished in *The Threepenny Review* and *Calyx*. Nair lives
in Brooklyn with her husband and daughter.

VIDEO

VIDEO

stories

Meera Nair

Anchor Books
A Division of Random House, Inc.
New York

FIRST ANCHOR BOOKS EDITION, MARCH 2003

"Summer" previously appeared in *Calyx*. "The Lodger in Room 726"
previously appeared in *The Threepenny Review.*

The Library of Congress has cataloged the Pantheon edition as follows:
Nair, Meera, 1963–
Video : stories / Meera Nair.
p. cm.
ISBN 0-375-42111-4
1. India—Social life and customs—Fiction. I. Title.
PS3614.A57 V53 2002
813'.6—dc21 2001036951
CIP

Anchor ISBN: 0-385-72103-X

Book design by M. Kristen Bearse

www.anchorbooks.com

Printed in the United States of America
10 9 8 7 6 5 4 3 2 1

For my parents,
and for Arun and Anokha

I ask you to pause and to hear it again,
but you sweep ahead to hear another music.
It's true we cannot live on echoes.

—NISSIM EZEKIEL

I am writing to you from your far off country . . .
that map of longings with no limit.

—AGHA SHAHID ALI

See, now they vanish,
The faces and places . . . to become renewed,
transfigured, in another pattern.

—T. S. ELIOT

Contents

VIDEO

Video

Naseer lay beside his wife in the dark and wished he had never seen that video. He blamed it for all the trouble they had been having lately. He knew Rasheeda was angrier than she had ever been in all their years of marriage. Ever since he first asked her the question, she had flung her silence at him. But that was only during the day, in front of the rest of the family. At night, after the children were asleep, she hadn't been so quiet. Now, with his blood cooling, he thought of mollifying her as he had done for many nights lately, and making her understand with clear, logical, unemotional explanations why he needed her to do this for him. She was his wife, for God's sake. He had rights, didn't he?

"Rasheeda! Listen—" he began.

"Fifteen years we've been married and now you want me to do this—this thing!" His wife sat up abruptly, reached for her nightgown, and thrust her head into it.

Oh God, here she goes again.

"Allah, please put some sense into this man. Is this a good thing to ask your wife to do? I've had three of his children and now he asks me for this . . ." Her voice was muffled but the aggrieved tone came through loud and clear.

She acts as if she has a Star TV channel blasting directly into Allah's living room. As if He's just waiting there, eager to listen to Madam Rasheeda. Naseer knew the situation was serious, but he couldn't help smiling in the dark.

"Allah, he has gone mad. His body's noise is louder than any voice of reason," Rasheeda continued.

Why does she talk so loud? Naseer twisted his head around to make sure the door to the children's bedroom was closed. She will probably wake the children and his brothers and their wives and his mother the way she's carrying on. Surely his brothers didn't have troubles like his: a recalcitrant wife who sat up in bed at night and belligerently talked to her God.

He looked at her now as she sat marooned in the middle of the bed. The light from the streetlamp filtered through the cotton curtains, turning her broad back pale blue. It was hot and still and Naseer shivered involuntarily as the sweat on his legs dried.

A few nights ago, he had even cited the teachings of the mullahs exhorting Muslim wives to listen to their husbands in all things. But then she was hardly the sort to be frightened by the mullahs, not with her direct line to Allah.

"But Allah, I'll tell you one thing. Never shall I submit to this man's whims. I'll do my duty as a wife, but where is it written that I have to do such things?" Rasheeda's monologue showed no signs of flagging.

That last bit was for his benefit, not Allah's, thought Naseer as he reached for his pajamas at the foot of the bed. And what was this about doing her duty as a wife? When she was in bed with him, she didn't just lie there hating it like some other women he had heard about. He should know. She liked the stroking and rubbing all right. Not that there had been too much of that lately. Take tonight. He hadn't cared to slip his hand down her body and finish her off. He'd asked her right in the middle of it all, gasping the question at her, shameless in his need. But once again she said no, shaking her head from side to side, her eyes tightly closed. So he had ended it quickly and not bothered with her at all. But it wasn't right, and he didn't like it. Naseer shifted uncomfortably on the far side of the bed. He liked his fingers being swallowed up in her slopes and ridges and bumps, in that hidden, miniature landscape all her own. He liked having her face turned up at him, her eyes gone far away to the place where her feeling was building. He liked her giggling, embarrassed because she thrashed about so much. She'd always giggled, ever since the first time, a few months after their wedding when he had finally stumbled on how to pull her across the threshold of fear and nervousness to pleasure.

Her complaints to Allah done at last, Rasheeda lay down, taking care to not brush against him in the muggy dark. Everything had been fine right until the moment he sat down on the black rattan chair in Khaleel's shadowed living room and the video player was turned on.

Naseer had gone over to his cousin Khaleel's place to ask his opinion about a new van he wanted to buy. He'd use it to deliver hardware supplies from his store to customers who phoned in their orders. One had to move with the times. Khaleel had his own auto repair shop and could pick out a bad vehicle from a good one by merely listening to the sound of its engine, like a doctor to a patient's chest. Nusrat, his second brother's wife, had called loudly after him from the kitchen window as he opened the gate and stepped out into the street. "It's kababs tonight, so don't be late. You know how Rasheeda won't eat without you."

Adnan, thin and gangly, with Rasheeda's fine, flyaway hair,

was playing cricket in the street in front of the house. After a quick sideways glance confirming that his father had stopped to watch him, he gazed seriously at the ball. Old Janaki Ram was sitting on his stoop in his striped undershorts, customary teacup in hand.

"Your boy is hitting four after four today," he said. Naseer smiled and rubbed at his beard to hide his pride.

A few minutes into Adnan's turn at the wicket, Naseer started down the street and Adnan lifted his hand off the bat for a second in farewell. Naseer fought an impulse to tell Adnan to go home before it got too dark. He was fourteen and Naseer didn't want to embarrass him in front of his friends.

The street barely managed to squeeze between the buildings that lined its length. The houses scrunched up against each other and in the shadows of the late evening they seemed to draw closer together, huddling over the street like gossipy old women. The houses around here had hardly changed from when his father's father had first moved in here. Naseer looked up affectionately at the lacy wooden balconies, their curlicued railings still overhung with the saris housewives had forgotten to take inside from the sun. As he walked he greeted the men resting from the heat on the porches, old men who, with the memories of his father still fresh in them, expected him to stop and inquire respectfully about the gout or kidney stones or un-employed son they suffered from.

Here and there transistor radios played softly, the tinny voice of Lata Mangeshkar singing a song about being stricken sleep-less by love. One stanza flowed into another, accompanying him from porch to porch all the way down until he turned the corner onto Khaleel's street.

Here the houses around him were newer. Bright white-washed walls shouldered up against worn stone flared and dimmed in the light of passing cars. A shiny black Fiat jutted out of a gate, taking up street space. Khaleel's place was the last one, just before the street curved away at an angle.

When Naseer got to the door the house was dark, yet he could see the TV's staccato flicker in the living room through the opaque windowpane. At his knock the TV was switched off. Khaleel took his time to answer the door.

"Oh! It's you. I thought it was Baba come back from Madras early," Khaleel said, wiping his palm down the front of his shirt.

Khaleel's father had a twenty-year-old property dispute that came up for a hearing every few years and took him away from home. The old man's tenacity had become a joke in the family.

"I rented a VCR for the day—thought I'd watch some films. You know how Baba is so strict and all, not allowing us to do anything." Khaleel moved aside to let Naseer in.

"All the women kissing men in broad daylight in front of the children, this TV sheevee will destroy the country yet . . ." Naseer mimicked his uncle's disgruntled old man's voice.

Khaleel didn't laugh as he usually did.

Looking at his cousin now, Naseer thought, as he had many times before, how strange it was that all the men in his family were short and wiry and bearded.

"So what're you watching? Anything with Amitabh in it?" Naseer loved the actor. When *Sholay* had been released, he had seen it five times.

"No," Khaleel said. "Come on in and see for yourself."

When Khaleel switched on the VCR, there were two foreigners on the screen—a woman and a man. The man lay on the bed and the woman knelt between his legs. White skin, golden hair, smooth nakedness. She bent down. Then she opened her mouth over him. After one frozen minute of incredulity, everything inside Naseer contracted. He put his hands over his stomach as if to contain the faint tremors he felt starting. He watched the woman, her movements sometimes languid, sometimes frenzied, her cheeks working. It was unbelievable that any woman would admit a man inside her face, to touch her tongue and her teeth and the inside of her cheeks. The two of them seemed bound together in some extreme ecstasy, the man watching the woman looking at him. They took a long time to finish. Watching the man as he arched on the bed, Naseer felt as if he was about to lose control and slide off the chair trembling and moaning—right there in Khaleel's mother's living room with its bright blue carpet and showcase filled with the ceramic dogs her daughter had sent from Dubai.

Naseer got up abruptly and mumbled something to Khaleel about coming back another time. Moving toward the door, Naseer saw himself reflected indistinctly on the TV screen, his shadowy form moving closer as he neared the set. Khaleel barely acknowledged his departure, and his eyes, glittering in the blue light, remained riveted on the screen.

Outside, Naseer leaned against the wall and breathed deeply. He could feel the rough stubble of its surface pressing against his shoulder blades and back through the thin muslin of his kurta. The wall was uncomfortably warm.

He couldn't bring himself to walk just yet, not with this hot weight in him, as if everything inside had descended to settle around his lower stomach and thighs. It was almost pain but not quite, he thought, shocked at the great scrabbling need that stretched down his middle. There had been a time when he was twenty-three and just married to Rasheeda when he could go four times a night. The greediness of a recent virgin—that's what it had been. The need had been a constant unfulfilled thrum in him. Now here it was again, as if someone had plucked hard at a taut string that ran from his head down to his toes.

When he finally pushed himself away from the wall and started walking home, he felt grateful that the old men on the stoops had gone inside to their dinners. He had heard the boys who hung around the college cafeteria snicker about things like this a long time ago, but it had always remained some mythic thing that occurred elsewhere, not in a home, not on an ordinary bed.

Back at home he found Rasheeda in the bedroom getting fresh nappies for the baby.

"Oof, oh! Husband! Stop it! Everybody's waiting for their dinner downstairs and you're doing nonsense things," she laughed, brushing him aside, a little surprised at his sudden ardor. Then she hurried away, the cloth triangles swinging from her hands.

He stood in the middle of the bedroom, reluctant to go down and face the clattering crockery and noisy children in the dining room. What if he rented a VCR and the film himself and got Rasheeda to watch it with him? No. It was impossible—the only TV they owned was in the living room and his mother watched *Understanding the Koran* on it in the afternoons, her silver head nodding sleepily, her fingers slipping now and then off her prayer beads.

At dinner Rasheeda caught him looking at her as she returned from the kitchen with a refill of the kababs and smiled absently in his direction. The oil from the biryani had left her lips slick and shiny. The older children, who had been fed earlier and sent into the living room, fought for control over the TV. Today was Wednesday and that meant *Baywatch*. Naseer knew his brothers would join the kids to watch the serial after dinner.

"Bhai-jaan must have snacked at Khaleel's—he's hardly eating anything at all," Nusrat announced archly. Everyone turned to look at Naseer and he had to nod yes and scramble to name a snack. He got up hurriedly from the table. Farhana stumbled up behind him and stood clutching desperately at his legs for an instant before plopping down onto her behind. She drew breath to wail. He picked her up and went into the living room to order his sons up to bed—he didn't want them watching half-naked women cavort on the beach.

The children bribed and nagged into going to bed and alone with his wife at last, Naseer could feel Rasheeda's pleased astonishment at his impatience.

"Wait, wait, let me turn off the light," she said, reaching for the lamp.

"No. Wait," he said. He put his hands on her hips and pulled her down with him on their bed. Then he pushed himself away from her and took a deep breath. "I saw this video at Khaleel's," he began and stopped. He wanted to say the words carefully, lucidly, even though whole sentences and phrases had jostled in his head all through dinner and the interminable conversation with his brothers afterward. "It was foreign and they were, you know, doing it." He felt embarrassed but determined. This had to be said.

"Allah! Cheee! Toba toba, so *this* is what you were doing," Rasheeda looked at him, her mouth contracting in disgust.

"Listen, I have never seen anything like this . . ." He pressed on. He told her about the video, about the woman and what she had done for the man. Just saying the words excited him. He felt relieved. Now she knew too. The knowledge of this disturbing, fascinating new thing was no longer in his head alone.

Rasheeda moved away and watched him gravely, warily,

as he struggled on, trying to explain the moment, the things he'd felt.

In the end, his telling ragged at the edges, he blurted out what he wanted. He knew, even as he stumbled over the words "me" and "mouth," that they came out all wrong, as if they were not meant to be said aloud between them there in their bedroom of fifteen years.

Rasheeda's face contorted in shock and she jumped off the bed as if the sheets were on fire. After a first strangled sound of surprise she stood silent.

"No." She said it quietly. Just that one word, thrown down firmly in front of him without any explanation attached. "No," she said again as she lay down heavily and turned her back to him, her nightdress rustling in the dark. Then, after a long silence in which he willed himself to calmness and was about to fall asleep—"Never."

From then on it had been the same story—every night a repetition of tonight. Her "no" was all-encompassing, leaving him without space to maneuver or argue. All she gave him was that word, and it stood steadfast against all his attempts to wear it down, as unassailable as a mountain made of glass.

Yet every day in his head the blonde woman's mouth stretched itself wide and pink over him and would not let him rest.

Sitting behind his counter in the hardware store, Naseer looked at the men who came in asking for hinges and light fixtures and wondered if he was the only man in the world who had spent all these years so pathetically ignorant of this pleasure. Surely all sophisticated men enjoyed it. It was his father's fault for forcing him to marry at twenty-three.

Naseer had wanted other things. Nodding over his college

books through the long, humid nights, he had imagined himself, standing bareheaded under a pitiless blue sky, building the dam that would put sweet water in the earthen pots of the villagers and green their fields. Just like Dílíp Kumar in the movie *Naya Daur*. But he was the eldest son, ordained to carry on the family business, and Naseer couldn't bring himself to break his father's heart. So, instead of Naseer, his brothers had become engineers. They were the ones who sat in high-ceilinged government offices, dusty with stacks of forgotten files, and approved plans to build other buildings exactly like the ones they worked in. Now, with his father gone, they accorded him the respect they would have given his father. It made him more distant than ever from them.

Naseer told himself he was deeply unhappy. The craving wouldn't let him be and he felt betrayed by this discontent. He had struggled to be pleased with his lot over the years. Even when he was forced to take on the business, he had taught himself to find satisfaction in the idea of some unknown house, somewhere in the city, growing older, held together by his hinges and latches and nails, the doorknobs pushed open day after day by children and the children's children, the curtains pulled back on his curtain rings. There was a kind of immortality in it. Now Rasheeda had spoiled it all. Why couldn't she behave as wives should?

Rasheeda started sending his breakfast out of the kitchen with Aliyeh, the youngest sister-in-law, who kept her sari-covered head bowed respectfully as she quickly set his omelet down on the table, poured his tea, and scuttled back into the kitchen. As if he was a guest who had overstayed his welcome, thought Naseer.

Ever since his mother had ceremoniously handed over the keys to her after Siddiq was born, Rasheeda had run the household. She had slid expertly into the role of matriarch, although she'd been barely thirty-one, as if she had practiced running a household of seven adults, five children, and three maids secretly over the years.

Nowadays, as she walked past him pretending to be busy with the children, he resented that she could always find things to do in the confused bustle of communal living. With his brothers, their wives, or the children always around, he could never get her alone. At night, he was usually asleep by the time she finished ironing school uniforms or discussing tomorrow's menu or whatever it was she did down there to delay coming upstairs.

Some nights he stayed awake, fighting sleep. But the more he tried to persuade her, the more adamantly she condemned this ungodly practice, vociferously calling upon Allah to intervene. Naseer couldn't stop asking either, couldn't just let it be. It's like an unending game, he thought. Only whatever move he made Rasheeda was already there, anticipating him, ready with her defense.

At mealtimes, Naseer imagined he could feel the eyes of the other women on him. Could Rasheeda have dared tell them about what was going on between them? She wouldn't, would she? Violate the quiet yellow warmth of their bed, throw it open for all to peer and comment? His thoughts brought on a great, bursting pressure in his chest.

Yet in the evenings he couldn't wait to get back home. It was a relief just to have Rasheeda somewhere nearby where he could at least watch her face. And her mouth.

When his parents had found him Rasheeda, he had said yes without a demur. It was his mother who had asked the marriage broker, "Do we really want such a highly educated daughter-in-law?" She had been uneasy with the fact that Rasheeda had passed high school. But his father had surprised him by insisting on the match.

Naseer saw Rasheeda on the evening of their wedding only after the Kazi, his interminable mumbling incantations finally done, decreed he could see the bride.

He had gone into the zenana, the women's hall, where she sat surrounded by her relatives and friends, the women whispering and shimmering around him in their yellow and green silks. One of Rasheeda's oldest aunts held a long-handled mirror under her bowed head, carefully angling it inside her dupatta so that he would see only her face and nothing else. He never forgot that first glimpse of her face framed by the veil, the mirror filled suddenly with large sloping eyes and pale pink mouth. Clumsy as he bent over to peer at the mirror, he had stepped on her skirt, and she had put her hand out quickly to tug the material away. Her hand had lain there for an instant, white and forlorn, before it retreated under her heavy, embroidered shawl. A faint, damp mark was left behind on the rose silk where she had touched it, and he was overwhelmed by a sudden compassion. He had wanted to tell her then not to worry—everything would be all right.

Sometime during the all-important first night, Naseer asked her to stand next to him and was surprised to discover that he was only half an inch taller than she was. In spite of her nervousness, she had laughed. The rest had come slowly, in awkward fits and starts. He was gentle with her and she patient with him. Just as he mapped her body, he cataloged her peculiarities—the faint, fair down on her legs, the way her arm pressed the pillow to her face in the morning, shutting out the day for a few minutes more.

Then the children arrived. First Adnan, then Siddiq, and the last one, Farhana, a wriggling, big-bottomed baby girl. Over the years they fit into each other. Now when he reached for her at night it was like driving down the road to the store. He knew when to take the curve, which pothole to avoid, and where to stop. He hadn't wanted much more. Until the woman in the video opened her glistening mouth.

It was the twelfth of June and Rasheeda's birthday. It was time they solved this impasse, he decided. He called in the afternoon and told her he had tickets to the latest Aamir Khan movie.

"How many?" she asked, her voice unsmiling on the telephone.

"Just you and me," he said firmly. On the rare occasions they went out to the movies or a restaurant, all the brothers and their wives would go together, piling into the old green van, everyone teasing Aliyeh, the youngest sister-in-law, forcing her onto her husband's lap.

When he went home to pick Rasheeda up, there were giggles from the kitchen. She sat quietly by him until he finished his tea and samosas. A woman's love can be measured by how many samosas she urges you to eat, he thought. She did not force any upon him this time.

"Good samosas. Okay. Let's go, the movie begins at six thirty," he said, all bluff and hearty, hoping she would play along, at least in front of the sisters-in-law, who looked over at them from time to time.

"Why this sudden good mood? This movie and everything?" Rasheeda didn't smile back.

She must know that he was trying to get back to where they were, before she'd stopped talking to him, he thought.

"Well, it is your birthday, isn't it?" he said. He had bought her a present but didn't want to give it to her in front of the other women. Nusrat would have had something catty to say for sure.

Rasheeda didn't answer, but she didn't argue either, just got dressed quickly and walked out with him, flinging a stream of instructions over her shoulder on what to give each of the children for dinner. On her silk sari, flowers spread over her breasts like purple hands.

The entire family came out, crowding around the gate to see them off. Farhana began to cry.

"Enjoy yourselves," Nusrat smirked. Aliyeh bent down and smoothed Rasheeda's sari over her calves one final time.

"It's not as if we're going away for three years, is it?" Naseer grumbled.

"Shh, it's okay. We don't go out alone together every night," Rasheeda said.

Back from the movie, Naseer stood in front of the mirror in their bedroom and drew Rasheeda to him.

"We still look nice, don't we?" he said. In her high heels, she was slightly taller than he was.

"I like your shorter beard," she said, so he rubbed it against her cheek. His hands stroked her wide hips and pulled her against him.

"I must do something about my weight," Rasheeda said, but he shook his head.

"Imagine if you were thin and bony like that heroine in the movie. I like large portions." He slipped his hands under her breasts and hefted them in the mirror. Rasheeda's hands came up to pull his away, but she was laughing, her face soft and forgiving.

Later, Naseer did all the things she liked: rubbing her back in widening circles, dragging his thumb slowly across her armpit. He took his time, teasing her, starting her up and slowing her down and starting her up again, until she was desperate and insistent against his palm.

Naseer lay awake for two hours after Rasheeda fell asleep. He felt hollow and dissatisfied. The lovemaking between them had been decent. But he couldn't help wondering how much better it might have been if she had lowered her mouth to him, taken him slowly into her mouth. He hadn't brought it up this time because he was afraid she'd stop talking to him again.

Next to him Rasheeda shifted onto her back. A few minutes later she started snoring softly. Naseer smiled. She was always indignant when he told her she snored, as if it were somehow his fault for even bringing it up. He put his hand on her shoulder. A push onto her side always made her stop. Not that she'd know or wake up. His mother liked to say that Rasheeda could sleep through an earthquake. Yet when Farhana was younger, she'd scramble up even when the baby just burped in her sleep. It was amazing how women could switch themselves off and on like that.

Rasheeda smacked loudly in her sleep and her mouth fell open. Watching her, Naseer felt himself become hard even before the thought was fully formed in his head.

He slid off the bed, his heart pounding. He walked around to Rasheeda's side, fumbling with the string of his pyjamas. Her mouth was slack and agape and she did not wake up even when he knelt awkwardly with his knees next to her face. He leaned far over her head and tried to direct his cock safely inside her mouth. His knees were trembling so hard that he had to grip the headboard with his other hand—even then he slid off the edge of the bed a few times. Then he was in. Was he touching the roof of her mouth?

Just then Rasheeda woke up and stared at him looming over her, his crotch in her face. In her shock Rasheeda's lips closed automatically over him. She made a strangled sound. He thought confusedly of pulling out, but he could not. Not then. Afterward, he couldn't remember when he thought she wouldn't mind or how he held her sleep-dazed head still and ignored her struggling. It was all over in seconds anyway. She got up, ran into the bathroom, and didn't come out for a long time.

I could have touched her brain if I'd wanted to, he thought, feeling excited and mellow at the same time. I was so close to where she lives, not somewhere down there far away; I was more inside her than I've ever been. Then he fell asleep even as he was thinking that he would never be able to sleep.

Rasheeda was still in the bathroom when he woke up in the morning. She hadn't come out even when he left for the store, three hours later. When he came back in the evening, Nusrat, who over the years had developed a certain degree of familiarity with him, took it upon herself to have a word with him. Rasheeda had stayed in the bathroom the whole day.

"She refuses to go to a doctor, says there's nothing wrong with her," she said, looking genuinely worried.

Rasheeda went to the bathroom twelve times the next day. Ten times the third. She did not stop frequenting the bathroom even after a week, yet she refused to see a doctor. Naseer, frightened for her life, even brought one to the house. The doctor, a small, skinny man who looked as if he'd received his degree only months ago, stood nervously in their bedroom, clutching his brown leather medicine bag to his crotch.

"I am fine, Doctor-saab, please go away," Rasheeda yelled from the bathroom.

"Get a *peer*. They know about these strange afflictions, this nonstop diarrhea and suchlike things," the doctor stuttered and fled.

Naseer couldn't bring himself to summon any sorcerers with their magic cures into the house. Maybe she would get better on her own, he thought.

But Rasheeda wouldn't stop. She claimed the outside bathroom for herself. It stood next to the small vegetable garden in the backyard and had been abandoned after the new bathrooms with concealed plumbing were built. She gave herself up to its white-tiled interior at regular intervals. Every hour on the hour, like the BBC. Right in the middle of tying bows in Farhana's hair, she would set her comb down and hurry to the bathroom. Halfway to the greengrocer's down the road, she would stop and head back to the house, overcome by her colon.

Yet nothing else seemed to be the matter with her.

Naseer could hear the sisters-in-law talking and laughing in the kitchen as he ate his breakfast alone. "The whole day she's in the bathroom, but she doesn't look sick or lose weight," they would say. "It is sort of unnatural, don't you think?"

He had to admit it was true. Rasheeda's plump white arms and open luminous face still looked as desirable as ever as she pushed past him, hurrying toward the bathroom.

Since Rasheeda didn't get any sicker, the household adapted quickly, resilient as always. This peculiar new bump was absorbed quickly and ironed flat into its texture. Rasheeda's vigils in the bathroom soon ceased to be an event and became part of her Rasheedaness, protected from comment by their very familiarity and repetitiveness. Even the children tired of shouting "She went ten times today" at him the minute he returned from work. His brothers didn't offer their irritating commiseration anymore.

The children came home from school and went straight to the outdoor bathroom, confident of finding Rasheeda there. They stood outside the door to talk to her.

"Gunjan stole my orange. I hate him," Siddiq would say. He hoarded complaints like sweets.

"The math teacher is horrible. You come and tell the principal that he shouldn't give us so much homework." Farida, Nusrat's little princess, could appeal only to Rasheeda, since her mother didn't believe in coddling children.

"I need ten rupees to pay the PT fees tomorrow." Even Adnan, his initial embarrassment forgotten, leaned against the outer wall of the bathroom and held shouted conversations with her.

"Never mind, I'll give you another orange tomorrow . . . Don't talk about your teacher like that. Have you no respect? . . . Adi, ask your father for the money." She'd answer each of them, serene and inviolate, firmly embedded in their world.

Gradually, as the days became weeks, even the vegetable sellers and fishmongers pushed their handcarts to the back gate near the bathroom and Rasheeda. They would lean over the gate and make their appeals.

"Fresh tomatoes, four rupees, Bibiji. Ekdum fresh!" the vegetable wallah would shout.

"Three is quite enough," Rasheeda would bargain with zest, and they'd give in easily, bemused by this new method of commerce.

"Only for you, Bibiji, don't tell anyone else, only for you three rupees." The transaction concluded, the vegetable wallah or fish wallah would go up to the kitchen and get the payment from Aliyeh or Nusrat.

For a time there was the problem of the keys. As the eldest daughter-in-law, only Rasheeda had the honor of carrying the keys to the pantry and the cupboards. Since the doors were kept carefully locked against the pilfering servants, Aliyeh and Nusrat had to trek down to the bathroom and Rasheeda every time they needed supplies.

One day Naseer saw Nusrat standing outside the bathroom door, tapping her foot impatiently. When she saw him, she muttered under her breath. The next morning Naseer sent a carpenter he knew to cut a small door in the center of the larger one. Rasheeda, temporarily out of the bathroom, said nothing, but she came out from the kitchen to watch him as he planed the sides of the small square of wood and attached hinges and a latch. She offered him tea when he was done, the carpenter reported when Naseer asked him, his voice as studiously casual as Naseer's. Naseer almost started to say that now all Rasheeda had to do was pass the key through the hinged door to whoever came knocking, but he caught himself in time. No need to add to the gossip that was surely circulating already. That evening Rasheeda brought Naseer his tea and set it on the table before him silently. He raised his head eagerly but she walked away before he could say a word.

One Sunday afternoon, when Rasheeda was taking her siesta, Naseer walked around the vegetable garden and, after making sure no one was watching, peered into the bathroom. It was hot inside the dingy room, with a thick, spongy heat that reflected down from the tin roof. On the ledge beside the commode were seashells, a bottle of glue and some pasteboard, someone's half-finished math homework, a recipe in Urdu, and the small transistor radio he had given her. She's destroying our marriage because she wants to listen to Hindi songs in the toilet, he thought. She had metamorphosed even as he watched, like the women in the fairy tales of his childhood, who turned into houris or winged ponies if a man dared to spy on them. Only he was dislodged. Everything else went on as normal. The TV was loud in the living room—the entire family was watching *Star Trek*. He couldn't understand the fascination with weird-looking space travelers. His life was in shambles; there were objects collapsing inside him, shivering apart like a dilapidated house struck by a cannonball, and they were watching TV.

Rasheeda had left his bed the second day after her visits to the bathroom began and now slept with the children, who were delighted; within minutes she had turned it all into an exciting game. Some nights he would hear them giggling behind the door in the other room.

Lying awake at night, he stared at the faintly luminescent square of the window and struggled to form the sentences he wanted to say to her in the morning. He would wake up and she would be gone, sucked into the everyday chaos of the household. He imagined himself marching into the kitchen to drag her out and confront her with the state of their marriage. But the thought of his sisters-in-law looking up aghast at him—the omnipotent, respected elder—made him cringe at the potential embarrassment of it all. In the meantime, Rasheeda continued to orbit around the toilet like a penitent devotee seeking absolution.

As the days passed, even the ladies of the neighborhood resumed their customary afternoon visits. They sat with their teacups in the shade of the tamarind tree in front of the bathroom and talked about other housewives who weren't there. Rasheeda would go in and out of the toilet, and the conversations would continue uninterrupted. Naseer had had the roof of the outhouse tarred so now it was a lot cooler inside.

Miriam, one of the young women down the road, had

started dropping in more frequently than the other house-wives. Her brand-new husband listened more to his parents than to her, she pouted, the color rising in her cheeks.

"It's as if I am nobody, just someone he can . . . you know . . . and then ignore." She caught the end of her blue du-patta between her teeth and stopped. The listening women sighed sympathetically. They knew.

One afternoon, Rasheeda called Miriam close to the door of the bathroom. Miriam smoothed a few strands of hair away and pressed her ear to the door. All the straining women could hear was a low mutter from inside. Miriam had a secret smile when she left. A few days later Miriam was back—all glow and giggles. Whatever Rasheeda had advised had worked like a charm. He's my little puppy dog now, Miriam crowed.

That was the beginning of it. Later, when there were lines of young women waiting to talk to Rasheeda in the bathroom, the original story was repeated proudly by Miriam. I was the first, she'd say, walking importantly through the small knots of women waiting to recount their troubles to Rasheeda. They told her things they wouldn't tell their best friends. Most of the talk was about husbands and in-laws, the trials and tribulations of living in joint families. Sometimes all some embattled girl wanted to hear was her own voice. They called Rasheeda *Sandaz Begum*—Madam Bathroom—affectionately. All she did was dispense commonsense advice. But the women kept coming back.

To Naseer this meant that he saw Rasheeda even less than before. She spent even more time in the bathroom. There were even more people who demanded her attention now. His mother, disgusted by the goings-on in the backyard, called him into her room and said some sharp words to him.

"Who does your wife think she is? Some kind of guru or

what? What is all this khoos-poos whispering with women in the backyard? Would your father have tolerated all this nonsense?" She spat a thick brown stream of tobacco into the silver spittoon beside her bed.

One Saturday, after he had spent an hour watching the women murmur in front of the bathroom from behind the curtains of his bedroom window, Naseer realized that each of these women had probably spoken longer with Rasheeda than he, her husband in the eyes of Allah, had in the past few weeks.

Rasheeda banned consultations on Sunday so she could do whatever she did in the bathroom in peace. When she came out to prepare the evening meal, he cut a four-inch-square out of one of the bathroom's wooden walls and covered the opening with steel mesh.

"It will make it easier for you to hear the women's complaints," he told Rasheeda the next day, putting his mouth close to the mesh. He had stood in line behind the women for twenty minutes. When they saw him, they hurriedly veiled their heads and shifted in embarrassment at having this man in their midst, not knowing whether to stay or leave. But he didn't move, not even when his brothers and their wives peeked out at him from the windows of the house. Now the children took their places, some standing on tiptoe to look over the balcony wall. Except Adnan. He had left the house the moment Naseer stepped into the back garden. As he got closer to the mesh, Naseer imagined Rasheeda looking at his face framed in the square, open and naked to her gaze in the sunlight. When he finally peered in, blinking from the sun, he could see only her dim form and little else in the gloom. She turned toward him abruptly, startled by his voice.

"Just wanted to make it easy for you to hear the women's complaints," Naseer repeated. She looked at him and said nothing. He thought he saw her nod. After a few moments Naseer left his place in the line and walked back to the house.

At dinner that night, Rasheeda reached across the table and heaped a ladleful of rice onto his plate. When Naseer looked up at her, she was looking back at him. Before she turned her face away to answer one of the children, he was quite sure he saw her mouth twitch gently at the corners.

The Lodger in Room 726

Chik-Chik and his plate of paranthas were about to cross the street. He had allowed the cars to breathe their warm gray puffballs of air on his ankles long enough. Suddenly he saw the opening. Now! Before the white Ambassador could nudge up to the Maruti again, he leaped into the traffic, slipping in a flash between cars, whipping around bumpers, crouching against a truck, staring for a scared instant into its greasy-hot, metallic underbelly. Then, pushing at the Cielo, holding it off easily with one hand, rushing, rushing, his feet unerringly finding the safe spaces amid the throbbing, panting engines, the cars and trucks and buses stopped just for a moment before they thrust forward again, eager to crush him and his paranthas. Then he was across, bursting out of the roadway, beating the cars and their loud complaining horns, to emerge shining and triumphant onto the sidewalk, his plate held aloft in victory, turning back to grin at them all, including the man in the maroon tie leaning out of his long car, looking at him in wonder, awestruck no doubt by his amazing expertise.

Chik-Chik stood on the sidewalk of the narrow citylane. It was squeezed between the tall, narrow buildings that held up a lopsided bit of sky. Across the street he could see the restaurant where he worked. He was carrying breakfast to the new Lodger in Komal Lodging and Boarding, the man in Room 726. There were brown betel juice stains at the corners of its landings. Chik-Chik especially liked the one on the second floor, the one that looked as if a tiger was smashing its head against the wall. He hoped it was still there. A few days ago Jano Bi, the cleaning lady, had washed away a stain that looked like a mountain with a melting peak. Chik-Chik was sure that he would have found many more rocks and cliffs on it if only he could have looked at it for some more time.

As Chik-Chik neared the new Lodger's floor he wondered if he would see him today. For fifteen days now he'd been bringing the Lodger his breakfast, and all Chik-Chik had seen of him was his hand. Long brown fingers and a steel-strapped watch, that's all he'd seen. As if that's enough, thought Chik-Chik, just to see a hand. I've seen hands and hands. What's so special about hands? Now a face, that would be something. How about a face? And why did the Lodger never go out? Maybe . . . what if . . . he's Nagarajan the pavement murderer. He could have run away from Bombay and come here, to Delhi. Hari, who was older than Chik-Chik and knew about these things, had once told him that the police hadn't ever managed to catch Nagarajan. He said Nagarajan went out after midnight and prowled among the poor people who slept on the sidewalk. Then, when the murderer spotted someone he didn't like, he'd pick up a stone, a big, heavy stone, and smash the person's head in. To think I've seen the hand that picks up those stones, thought Chik-Chik. But he would have taken off that steel watch before he did it, wouldn't he? Who would want scratches on a nice watch like that?

Chik-Chik stood outside the Lodger's door and shouted, "Saab, your breakfast."

If only he could see what this Nagarajan looked like today.

If only he could catch one tiny glimpse of this real-life murderer, this smasher of heads.

"Sir, your breakfast," he shouted again, putting his plate down at the Lodger's door.

Then he walked away to the end of the corridor, slapping his rubber flip-flops loudly on the floor. He'll think I've gone away, thought Chik-Chik, and quickly slipped his feet out of the straps. He was quieter than a lizard on the wall as he turned around and ran back up the corridor on his toes, thin, fair arms outstretched for balance, his oversized brown shirt floating in a fat T around him. He was headed for the stairway to the left of the lodger's door. He wouldn't be seen there, he thought. The door cracked open just as Chik-Chik was sailing past it.

It was the Lodger. Chik-Chik froze, tottering on his toes like a giant praying mantis. The Lodger stared at Chik-Chik in surprise. Chik-Chik stared back. Then the Lodger laughed underneath his mustache—a soft, abrupt laugh. The Lodger was tall, gangly, and light brown. Brown and lustrous like a gulab jamun soaked in sugar syrup. Now he half-leaned against the door and pondered the plate of paranthas as if he'd never seen it before.

"Wait a few minutes and you can take the empty plate back to the restaurant," the Lodger said, bending down at last to pick up his breakfast.

Ai! How did he know I'm from the restaurant, thought Chik-Chik. Maybe he's been watching me all these days. Chik-Chik searched the door for cracks large enough for a man to peer through.

Behind the door sunlight exploded into the room from open windows. The light glinted off the latch on one of the boxes, catching Chik-Chik's eye. There were seven boxes stacked on the table at the far side of the room, square wooden boxes, each the size of the ledger in which his boss recorded the sales every day, each locked with a tiny steel lock. Two of the boxes were old, brown, and chipped, while the others were brand new, the wood still cream-colored and shiny. That must be where he keeps his stones, thought Chik-Chik. Surely, each of the boxes would easily hold two or three fair-sized stones. And an expert murderer like Nagarajan would carry his favorite stones around with him, wouldn't he? Especially the big, pointy ones he used to pound people's heads in?

"What's in those boxes, sir?" Chik-Chik asked the Lodger.

"My work," he replied, coming to the door to return the steel plate, the bright disk suddenly flashing white light into the dim corridor. "Are you the boy who brings my food every day?" asked the Lodger.

Chik-Chik nodded. The Lodger handed him a five-rupee note. "Thank you," he said, in English.

Wait till I tell Hari, thought Chik-Chik. Wait till I tell him that I've got five rupees and that I've seen Nagarajan and the boxes with stones. In his hurry to get back to the restaurant, Chik-Chik forgot to walk down the steps backward as he usually did.

The five rupees went into Chik-Chik's tin trunk. It was his very first tip. As a cleaner of tables he wasn't entitled to tips. Hari, who was old enough to serve in the restaurant, saved up the fifty paisa or seventy-five paisa that customers left behind in the round blue plastic bowls they got their bills in. Chik-Chik's job was to wipe tables. After one set of customers had eaten he'd go around with his big yellow sponge and carefully swipe the spilled food off the tables into his basin. If new customers were already seated he would be especially careful, particularly at the edges of the table. Two years ago Chik-Chik had carelessly dripped water onto a big truck driver's trousers and he had hit Chik-Chik very hard on the side of his head. Chik-Chik's ear had buzzed and squeaked for days after that.

The owner of the restaurant would hit him sometimes too, one fat fist holding Chik-Chik's hands, the other one going *slap slap* against his face and shoulders. He'd hit Chik-Chik automatically, his eyes half-closed in his fleshy face. Chik-Chik thought that he often looked really bored when he did that. Ever since he'd turned twelve last August, Chik-Chik had stopped crying. Hari had said that big boys didn't cry.

That night, as Chik-Chik watched Hari cut out yet another picture of his favorite actress to put on his part of the wall, he told Hari about the Lodger, about his being Nagarajan the murderer, and about the wooden boxes in his room. But Hari didn't say anything. He was practicing his wolf whistle, strutting back and forth in front of his heroine. So Chik-Chik decided not to tell him that the Lodger had hair on his shoulders unlike any other man he had ever seen. Or that his black hair was short and spiky with little bits that stuck up straight from the back of his head like small, soft horns.

"Why are you called Chik-Chik?" asked the Lodger.

"Because that's my name. That's how they called me—the customers, when I first started working." Chik-Chik clicked his tongue against his teeth loudly, making the familiar *tsk-tsk* sound. "They would either call me that or Boy. I liked Chik-Chik better."

"So you named yourself," the Lodger said. "You are probably the only person in the world with that name."

Chik-Chik thought about that. Actually, he hadn't yet met anyone with the same name. But there were three Haris on his street alone.

"Chik-Chik . . . Chik-Chik." The Lodger said the words again and again under his breath, rolling the words like seeds in his mouth.

He was smiling. Chik-Chik decided he liked the way the Lodger said his name.

He had come up to see the Lodger on his afternoon break. The restaurant closed at 2:30 in the afternoon on Sundays and reopened in the late evening. He began stepping from one square of sunlight on the floor of the Lodger's room to another. It was a recent game. The floor felt warm, then cold, then warm again. Chik-Chik glanced in the Lodger's direction quickly. He was lying on his bed as usual. He lay on his bed with his eyes closed a lot. Maybe he was sick. Maybe he had cancer and was going to die. Chik-Chik had heard that cancer was a really bad disease. You caught it if you smoked and drank liquor. But the Lodger did not smoke or drink. So he couldn't have cancer, could he? Chik-Chik stopped hopping about and went and sat down next to the bed, as close to the edge as he could, without touching the Lodger. He counted his tips again. The Lodger had given him two rupees every day since that first day. He now had forty-five rupees. Chik-Chik carried the money with him everywhere. He liked having it close to him in his pocket, not locked up on the other side of the road in his iron trunk.

Chik-Chik looked around the room. He wondered if he had forgotten anything. The Lodger's shoes had been shined and put back in their place under the sink. This morning he had finally succeeded in bringing the cobbler's charge down to seventy-five paisa per shoeshine. He also had the Lodger's other shirt ironed. It lay on the table now, a pale blue square. The Lodger had told Chik-Chik not to do all these things for him, but he did them anyway. Chik-Chik got up from the floor and went over to the table to smell the shirt. The faint burnt smell from the hot coal iron was all mixed up with the Lodger smell. His Cuticura Talc smell. The Lodger dusted the talcum powder on his armpits every morning, raising his arms high, twisting his head to look at his underarm. He would shake the orange-and-white Cuticura Talc tin exactly as some customers shook the plastic saltcellar over their food. A few days ago the Lodger had held open Chik-Chik's shirt pocket with his finger and half-filled it with Cuticura powder. He had laughed looking at Chik-Chik's face.

The Lodger was strange that way, thought Chik-Chik. Sometimes he'd be happy and laughing.

"So what else has Jano Bi found out about the tenant in two-oh-five? Is he really a famous, bankrupt singer from Bombay?" he would tease Chik-Chik.

Other times he didn't speak, and would just lie on his bed. When he was quiet he wrote his letters, scribbling on blue inland envelopes, the ones that had to be folded three times before sealing. He'd write sitting silently in his chair, ignoring Chik-Chik, placing the envelopes carefully on the table to avoid the crack that ran across it like the branch of a tree.

Then one day the Lodger took him to a movie. He'd asked Chik-Chik who his favorite actor was. Chik-Chik had said Sunil Shetty, and even demonstrated Sunil Shetty's sky-high kicks for him. So they went to a Sunil Shetty film. Chik-Chik borrowed Hari's red T-shirt. It came down to his knees but at least it was new. It had a blue label on the pocket that said CHAMP in English. Hari could read English but he didn't know what it meant.

"Nowadays you are always hanging around that lodger fellow," Hari said. Hari sounded angry. But he had given Chik-Chik the T-shirt anyway.

Chik-Chik and the Lodger sat side by side. Chik-Chik carefully aligned his arm with the Lodger's on the armrest. He felt proud. And nervous. Was he laughing too loudly at the funny scenes? But then he heard the Lodger laugh loudly too, in reassuring, short coughs of laughter. The Lodger bought him a packet of salted peanuts in the interval. Later Chik-Chik told Hari that he couldn't be sure one hundred percent, but he thought it was the best evening of his life.

The more he visited the Lodger's room, the more the boxes tortured Chik-Chik. In that big, bare room washed clean by the sunlight, they were the only secret. Bolted and locked, they hoarded mysteries. They held answers to questions Chik-Chik dared not ask. In his mind the room's focus shifted to the corner where the boxes were. He wandered around them in ever narrowing circles, moving as close as he dared, even touching them quickly when he thought the Lodger wasn't looking. But the question refused to go away. One day the question wouldn't fit inside his mouth anymore and asked itself. After the words were said Chik-Chik could not speak, silenced by his own audacity and anticipation.

The Lodger did not say anything. But he looked at Chik-Chik's face for a long time. Then he got up and walked to his suitcase deliberately, unhurriedly. He took out a key ring. I bet there are seven keys for seven boxes, thought Chik-Chik, his stomach tightening in excitement. The Lodger carefully set all the boxes in a row on the table. Then he opened every lock and unfastened every latch. Finally the Lodger flipped back the lids of each box quickly, his body blocking Chik-Chik's view. He stepped away from the table and beckoned the boy closer.

The boxes were filled with marbles. They lay in rows embedded in white cotton, like frozen bits of rainbow. All the sunlight in the room seemed to have run in and pooled inside the boxes. Their colors screamed and whispered. They were translucent blood red, saturated cobalt blue, pale, pale green like the water at the edge of a pond. Some were glossy and shimmering, glowing as if they had tiny bulbs inside. Others were opaque, milky white and pink, or matte yellow like boiled egg yolk. There was even a wicked black one.

Their icy, smooth colors slid into Chik-Chik's eyes, his head, his nostrils, his throat, and his stomach. He walked the few steps toward the table in a daze, not taking his eyes off the marbles, like a devotee immersed in his God. He put his hand out blindly toward them and didn't see the Lodger flinch, didn't hear his soft "No." Chik-Chik lightly traced his fingers over each semicircle, traveling the short, cotton-covered distance between two marbles to crest the next one. That first time, that was all he wanted. Then he stepped back.

"I am going now," he said.

Suddenly he felt tired and spent from too much emotion. He went out quietly, still lost inside some newly discovered landscape. The next day and all the days after, whenever he came with the breakfast, Chik-Chik would ask to see one of the boxes.

"Open only one," he'd insist, pointing to the box of the day.

The Lodger picked up one of the marbles, a deep ruby red one, and held it up to the light. He said it was one of the best marbles he had ever seen. Chik-Chik looked at the marble as it rested in the Lodger's fingers. The sunlight seemed to be trapped there for that instant, sealed within the fragile red marble. Inside the marble was a bubble edged with red so dark it was black, an elongated oval captured within that other roundness. An eye within an eye. Red within red. Scattered around it were other, lesser bubbles, a whole galaxy of them suspended in the space between the Lodger's thumb and forefinger. Chik-Chik, unthinking, reached out and closed his fingers over the marble, over the marble and the hand of the man who held it up to the light.

The Lodger sold marbles to the big toy shops in Connaught Place and South Extension. That was how he made his living. Sometimes he got up to 500 rupees for them, he said. Chik-Chik, who had never seen 500 rupees, thought he was lucky that he could play with the marbles without paying for them. Somehow that made them even more precious. Two weeks after Chik-Chik had seen the marbles for the first time, one of the boxes got sold. It had green marbles with yellow veins and mottled blue ones that reminded Chik-Chik of a picture he had in his trunk of the earth with its oceans and dark green forests. There had been a black-and-orange-striped one that looked like an evil boiled sweet. All of them were gone, sold in some big bazaar by the Lodger. Chik-Chik avoided looking at that missing space on the table. To think he would never see those marbles again, he raged. Would all the other boxes be sold too? And then the Lodger would leave, wouldn't he?

Some nights, after he had washed the dishes and wiped the floor of the restaurant, Chik-Chik would climb up to the roof of the building. He'd lean against the water tank, gripping the pipes hard, hauling himself up against the wall to look over it. On the other side of the street, Komal Lodging and Boarding would be dark except for a few lighted windows. Chik-Chik would find the Lodger's window and if he waited long enough he'd see him—a tall, faint shadow against the glass. Chik-Chik would wait until he switched off the light and then he would go down to bed.

———

Whenever he could snatch a few moments away from the restaurant, Chik-Chik would run up to the Lodger's room. He would push open the door quietly in the morning and find the Lodger standing with knees bent and feet apart, doing his breathing exercises on the dingy balcony. Or Chik-Chik would look in on him late at night. He would rush in and go straight to the boxes, checking to see if they were all there. Then he'd look around quickly for the Lodger, as if he too was one of the boxes to be accounted for, before leaving as abruptly as he came in, racing down the steps, descending once again into the dark growl of the street. One Sunday afternoon when Chik-Chik got to the room the door was open. He stood quietly in the doorway and watched the Lodger. He was asleep on his bed, one arm hanging down almost touching the floor beside him. His short-sleeved shirt was pulled up, bunched into his armpit. Chik-Chik's eyes followed the sloping, dipping curve of the arm, the slight rise at the biceps and the narrowing at the elbow. In the crease of the arm a thick blue vein showed. As he watched it pulsed in a single slow beat.

That night Chik-Chik dreamed that the Lodger lay, his eyes closed, in the middle of the room. Chik-Chik worked over his body carefully. He placed marbles in the sockets of his eyes and in his open mouth. He filled the pockets of his collarbones with red and green marbles and heaped them on his stomach in fistfuls. Marbles erupted all over the Lodger's body as if rubies and diamonds that had lain dormant beneath the surface had pushed through to bloom like a spectacular, enticing pox on his skin.

———

Finally, after Chik-Chik had pleaded for days, the Lodger allowed him to help in the weekly ritual of polishing the marbles. Chik-Chik sat on the bed, bursting with excitement and pride, an open box balanced carefully on his knees. Three other boxes, their lids raised, lay beside him. The Lodger held out a marble to him and Chik-Chik leaned forward to reach for it. The box on his knees began tipping over. Frantic to save it before it fell, Chik-Chik flailed about and overturned yet another box. It seemed as if the marbles would never stop falling. They spattered like giant raindrops on the floor. They bounced and spun and rolled, little bits of rotating color. A few chipped and cracked, revealing dull, frosted insides. The Lodger groaned, a muted sound in the sudden chaos of the room. He began scrambling about, desperate to save as many from damage as possible.

Chik-Chik panicked, chasing first one marble then another across the room, crawling under the cot, searching in the corners. He slipped on the marbles and fell, got up, then slipped again. The Lodger grabbed him and held him close, struggling to remain upright. In his arms Chik-Chik stood still, his face pressed into the Lodger's chest, his own chest concave against the Lodger's stomach. The Lodger's arms fell away from Chik-Chik's shoulders almost immediately, but Chik-Chik did not move. He could not. He slid his palms slowly down the Lodger's arms. The Lodger began pushing him away playfully. Then he looked down at Chik-Chik's face. The Lodger stepped back, deliberately pulled Chik-Chik's hands off his body, and placed them back against the boy's side.

"Chik-Chik," he said. "Chik-Chik," he repeated, louder this time.

Chik-Chik's face returned from some warm place. He stayed where he was, unable to do anything but watch the Lodger, who had moved away from him and now stood at the window looking down at the street. He stood there for a long time. He would not look at Chik-Chik or smile. He did not seem to care about the fallen marbles either. Finally, Chik-Chik bent down to pick up the marbles once more.

"Go home, Chik-Chik," the Lodger said. He looked sad and tired. Chik-Chik thought he sounded angry. But he touched Chik-Chik gently on his shoulder. "Go home now," he said again.

When Chik-Chik took breakfast up to the Lodger the next morning the door was open. Inside, the mattress was rolled up and placed neatly against the far end of the bed. Chik-Chik walked up to the sink and looked under it. The Lodger's shoes were not there. He turned and looked at the stand next to the bathroom, but the Lodger's shirts were gone. The boxes of marbles were gone too, leaving only clean squares on the dust of the table. The room looked like every other unoccupied room in the lodge. Empty, bare, unfamiliar. Chik-Chik stood in the middle of the room with the Lodger's breakfast and wondered where to set it down. Finally he remembered and put the plate outside the door. He looked at his hands holding the plate and they were trembling. He stood with his head lowered and watched his hands for a long time. Then he walked over to the open window and rested his head against its frame. Far below him on his street, the cars and trucks looked small and ordinary. As he gazed down, the moving specks melted and ran together until they were no longer red or blue or green, but just colorless streaks that streamed away from him like tears and disappeared somewhere beyond the end of the street.

The Sculptor of Sands

When Jesu D'Costa stumbled over the twisted end of silk sticking out of the sand, he had been walking for half an hour in a world that was utterly without light. A lopsided moon had traveled alongside his bus from town, but by the time he stepped off, the clouds had smothered its radiance. Even the sea below the dunes had emptied into the night's blackness. Jesu had to concentrate on the dimmed froth that edged the water to decipher where the waves ended and the land began. When he tripped he did not curse. He was a good Catholic boy and he dreaded having to say the one hundred Hail Marys the priest handed out like candy after confession every Sunday. After a few moments he sat up and felt around for his foot to free it. Surprised by the unexpected luxury of the slippery silk against his palms, he tugged at it gently, and then walked forward, gathering loop after loop of the material as it reeled off the ground into his arms, the sand whispering off its surface, until its far end caught and stopped responding to his urging. Bewildered, he stood still under the dark sky, yards of silk billowing against his bare shins. Then the moon wandered out of the clouds and the night whitened enough for him to see that the final length of the sari was held fast under the half-buried body of a dead woman.

Jesu dropped his end of the sari in shock and the breeze stretched it out like a slim undulating flag. He crossed himself automatically and then stood above the body in a stupor while the moonlight grew stronger and the waves below spilled slivers of light onto the shore. He stared at her for so long that eventually her body assumed form and line and the familiar solidity of a human being. She lay in a narrow indented cradle the winds had carved out of the beach as if at home in the privacy of her bed, her hips, thighs, and tilted ankles easy and relaxed under the thin skin of sand. Fine sand had sifted into her curved and hollowed places, but had left her pale face and high breasts naked to the sky.

Struggling to see her clearly in the moonlight, Jesu remembered the torch he always carried. Although Jesu had walked this narrow stretch of the Goan coastline for most of the sixteen years of his life, he also knew the sea and its sly ways of scaring the unwary traveler. He liked to be prepared. He switched the torch on with his free hand and jerked the trapped end of the sari out from under the woman. She slid deeper into the hollow and the sand rushed in tiny cataracts off her suddenly animated arms. When his heart slowed, Jesu knelt down beside her resting place to shine the light full upon her.

A few strands of her long black hair, freed of the confining sand, blew about her face, loose and lively in the salt breeze. By the yellow light of the torch he saw her thin black eyebrows and slightly parted lips, and the faint brown mole at the left corner of her small mouth. He threw the beam lower and the narrow bones of her shoulders, the soft downcurve of her breast and the clean dip of her navel emerged out of the darkness, as if they had not existed until his weak circle of torch light brought them into being. When he brushed away the sand that encrusted her like powdered sugar, her skin had the sheen found only in the insides of half-shells. It left Jesu breathless. She wore a band of beaten gold on her left ankle and a purple bruise like a thread near her throat, as if some rough thief had begun to tear the jewelry off her but had been frightened away. She looked refined and except for that one bruise, unblemished. She looked as if she was not from around here, but from another place far away, Jesu decided. A place where women plaited silk for amusement and ate sweets made from clotted cream. He was sure that she never sat, even for a day, in a sun-stricken market in front of a pile of stinking fish with her sari hitched up to her thighs, like the women of his village. A small pale crab skittered across her toes and Jesu brushed it away. It brought him out of his dreaming. He looked up at the bleached sea and sky, the crisp line of the horizon. Dawn.

Jesu scrambled up from his place at her feet and started gathering the debris scattered around—the dried seaweed, fallen coconut leaves, and hardy beach ferns that trailed here and there along the dunes. He worked frantically, racing against the growing light, and strewed her with the leaves and fronds as if they were funeral flowers. He carefully smoothed sand over the foliage and left her, the most beautiful woman he had ever seen, buried under the sand in a place only he of all the men in the world knew how to find again. Then, the folded sari tucked under his shirt, Jesu ran the rest of the way and arrived at his village just as the first fishermen were raucously casting off to sea.

Years and years later, the story of Jesu and the woman became transformed into legend, and the tourist guides sold it every day for a fixed fee of five rupees to the pink-and-white Germans and long-haired Americans. They'd say that it was about then, right after Jesu had found the woman, that he became a sand sculptor. But even then the women had different tales to tell. When the monsoons drove the tourists off the beaches and their men out of the sea, the women, with no fish to sell, wove baskets on their porches and told each other stories. Jesu shaped sand even when he played naked in his mother's backyard, they'd say, cracking roasted tamarind seeds between their teeth. Remember the statue of the Virgin Mary Mother of God he made when he was seven? Fatima, his mother, nearly fainted when she saw the Holy Mother rising out of the sand by her door when she returned with her unsold fish. She swore she saw the Virgin's veil move in the weak light of that June evening.

In the end it did not matter whether he was or wasn't a child prodigy—everyone who stepped onto that stretch of beach knew Jesu as the only villager who could conjure statues from the sand.

But these legends came later, after Jesu disappeared from the village.

In the days after he found the dead woman, Jesu went out to sea with the rest of the men. In his village, even the finest sculptor had to earn a living. The older fishermen laughed at him.

"Don't hike your lungi too high, Crazy Jesu," they'd tease him as he clambered onto the fishing boat, his bony legs bared almost to his crotch. "Or some big shark will eat your little shrimp."

Sebastian, the head rower, would shake his head in mock sadness over him. "It doesn't matter. He's not going to keep a woman anyway, even though he likes to think he's an artist. Women like a big ladle to stir their porridge, not a tiny spoon like the one he's got."

Jesu would concentrate on staying upright at his end of the boat and say nothing. Once, Tall Francis hit him on the side of his leg, supposedly by mistake, and knocked him off the boat into the sea; even then, Jesu held his tongue. When the boats returned and the women left for the market with their catch of gasping mackerel, he'd slip off to the stretches of beach far away from the nets and boats of the village. There he would dig his hands deep into the beach and fashion marvels in the sand: a pair of wide curly-toed shoes which stretched for many yards and held eleven of the littlest children if they stepped in gingerly and stood in a straight line; a whole city with minarets, tunnels, and towers, with steep steps leading to secret rooms; a procession of helmeted men marching nap-headed slaves along the spray-wet sides of the sand dunes only to disappear around a corner; and a hundred other scenes, all of which were washed away by the high tide.

In the evenings his father grumbled into his beard. Jesu had left the nets unstitched. Jesu had forgotten to gather driftwood for the fire. Jesu was never around, where did the boy go at night?

"Leave the boy alone . . . Don't you see what he does with the sand?" Jesu's mother would shush him. And his father would try to find forgiveness in his heart for his strange son by reminding himself of the money foreign tourists often left beside Jesu's creations.

Jesu didn't look up when the white girls stood beside his work making bird sounds, their rupees crumpled in their hands. He concentrated instead on the things the sand whispered in its wet, grainy voice into his palms. Only sometimes, when he couldn't bear the scent of faraway places that rose from the smooth bellies and bare ivory thighs so near his bent head, did he plunge panting into the cool forgiving sea.

His audience tripled after he started sculpting the women.

The first one was a mere suggestion of femininity, just a few meandering lines, something familiar in the curve of the sand. No eyes or nose or breasts. The statue that came after was veiled, her face barely visible underneath a lacy mantilla of sand. Yet there was something about the way she sat, resting against the dune she was carved out of, some grief in her face bent away from the sea, some indefinable emotion in the angle of her shoulders that spoke to the women who stopped by.

The village women who came to look at her, women who had not stopped working since they were taught to gut a sardine with pudgy four-year-old hands, sighed with a sadness they could not name. Because they could not think of the big things, they thought of how the rocks around the village pierced their children's feet; they felt again the yearning in their young brothers' voices when they'd sung the mando so long ago; they remembered the fathers and uncles and the young men with strong arms they had lost to the sea; and they wept. Soon it became a common sight to see a village woman standing in front of one of Jesu's statues, sobbing uncontrollably. As for the white girls, a few of them who saw the statues were struck with so much longing for the snow-heavy hedges and peaceful kitchens of their hometowns that they went back to their run-down hotels, packed their flowered skirts and beads, and took the next flight out.

At night, feeling better for their weeping, some of the women secretly thought of Jesu's hands. He was a mere boy still, they thought, yet his hands knew the things a woman feels: the deep-down quiet, angry, anguished, loving, naughty, doubting, cruel, womb-tickling churnings that they told no one else, not even their sisters. Surely his hands understood more than sand. Otherwise he would not have known how to put that question in the eyebrows of his sculpted women or the defiance in the rise of their breasts or the longing in the corner of their smiling mouths. So the thoughts of the women went, until the older married ones sighed and fell asleep.

But the younger, bolder ones who hadn't yet learned to give up orbited around him. The whirlwind in their hearts reined in with a smile, they offered to repair the rip in his shirt or make him chicken shakuti. When he ignored them they vowed to hate him forever and then came back the next day to watch his fingers caress the sand.

In the evenings, as they sat on their porches and oiled each other's hair, the girls retold their stories about Jesu. He never slept, because the sand talked louder at night and only he could hear it. He never drank feni like the other men because it was supposed to rot the heartstrings and everyone knows you couldn't be an artist with an imploded heart. He'd been walking toward the dunes late one night, Manuela said. She had seen him when she'd woken up and gone outside to pee. Of all the stories, only Manuela's was true, but fortunately for Jesu nobody believed her, because she was enormously fat and desperately wanted friends. So no one else actually saw Jesu slip away at night to go to the beautiful woman who waited for him in his secret place in the dunes.

No one saw him place a string of coral around her throat to cover the bruise or watched as he wrapped the silk sari over her nakedness. No one smelled the jasmine he wove into her hair to tame it. No ears heard the words he crooned to her every night. She was more beautiful than ever, as if the more he buried and uncovered her, the more the sand polished her into radiance.

The situation went on much the same for months and would have stayed the same, because nothing had really changed in the village for at least half a century. Except that the sighs of their women dreaming about Jesu finally wafted into the men's sleep and made them insanely jealous. The rumors grew ugly green wings and talons and flew around the village faster. Now it became easy to believe Manuela's stories; the men crowded around her house and only fell silent when Jesu passed by. Some spat and made the sign of the cross behind his back. Then a man who used to go out to sea with Jesu died of a fish-bone in his throat and that was enough for Tall Francis.

"You are bad luck," he said, when Jesu showed up at dawn. "Find another boat."

There was talk of witches who possessed young men lost on the beaches at night and the devil who sat by the well disguised as an impeccably dressed old man and other deliciously dire stories, until Father Masceranhas thundered his disapproval at Sunday Mass.

Jesu was summoned before the village Panchayat and told by the elders that he had to stop his sculpting if he wanted to stay on in the village. It made the women long for things they could not have and that was not a good thing, the old men of the People's Court decreed. Did he know that some of them had even started talking back to their husbands and fathers? Jesu heard the verdict quietly, but the women felt a great sad-ness settle upon them. To some it felt like they were seven again, the year they said goodbye to their childhood. Jesu's mother sobbed quietly in her hut and swore that she would never make the bibinca his father so loved ever again.

After the meeting, the men of the Panchayat convened at Aunty Esmeralada's for a few shots of feni, as was the custom.

"At least he wasn't making naked women on the sands," one fellow with few more teeth in his mouth than the others said after a few rounds.

The rest of the men agreed that Jesu had maintained propriety, and as the afternoon wore on and Aunty brought out plates of fried spicy sausage, they started feeling mellow and forgiving. They traded stories of Jesu as a small boy. Soon they were so full of good feni and reminiscence that when Jesu arrived in their midst at five o'clock, they welcomed him with friendly punches.

He had a request, he said, when the old men quieted down. He would like to make one last sculpture, just one more if the sirs would be so kind. The elders looked at each other in silence for a while. Each waited for the other to speak. Then the jolliest one threw his hands in the air and roared, "Why not? What harm can it do?" And all the others agreed that Jesu could go ahead.

"We'll even come and see it," they offered.

The news of Jesu's last sculpture flew around the village and the women looked at each other and smiled. The thought of crying one more time in front of a sand statue formed by Jesu's hands made it hard for them to sleep that night. In the morning they dressed up as if the Feast of Saint Francis Xavier had come early and started for the far reaches of the beach.

The men too decided to take a look before getting the boats out. The crowds walked along the beach looking for a shape in the sand. When Manuela and the other girls found her they didn't know whether to stay or cover their eyes and run away. In their confusion they stood there until the rest of the crowd surged up.

The statue lay just a few feet away from the edge of the sea. Her nakedness was carved out of the sand with such care paid to softness and flatness and roundness that she instantly became the most beautiful woman the people had ever seen. The anklet around her foot was so perfectly crafted that they could see the links that held it together, and the flowers Jesu had molded into her hair looked delicate enough to wilt under the early morning sun. The people stood and looked and could not turn their eyes away from the length of her slim fingers or the sweep of her cheekbones.

The men felt it first. A great wash of sorrow that they would never know such a woman rose from deep inside their bellies and left the taste of dried leaves in their mouth. And the women thought of the days long gone when they had looked at themselves in every mirror and windowpane they walked by, and wept into their lace handkerchiefs. In their grief they looked around for Jesu, hoping he had the answer to the questions they could not pry off the roofs of their mouths. But Jesu was not to be found.

No one saw him watching from his place high above them, hidden in the dunes. The people stood and stared at the statue of the woman until their feelings became too much to contain. At a particular moment all of them sighed together, a sigh of such depth and intensity and feeling that it dragged the far waves of the coming high tide off the surface of the sea earlier than usual. When the gathering waters first touched her outstretched fingers the people didn't know what to do. A few of the women moved forward instinctively and then drew back embarrassed—she was sand, after all. Some of the men at that very moment noticed that her breasts were shamelessly upthrust and that there was a kind of wanton abandon in her sprawl. They muttered under their breath.

When the first big wave curled over her a sneaking sense of relief came over the crowd. Then the waves foamed too close to their church shoes and the fathers and mothers gathered up their bemused children and moved away from the water's edge.

Amid the confusion, only Jesu and Manuela actually saw the wave that cradled her off the beach. When the crowd noticed and looked up, shading their eyes against the glare of the water, the statue was farther away, swaying gently in the swells that rolled in. Some of the women who lingered claimed to have seen the statue, a long slim shape on the surface of the water, long after the sand it was made from should have dissolved to the bottom of the sea. Later, in their beds at night, the men convinced them that they had imagined it. Only Manuela stuck to her story and swore to her dying day that she had seen a pale creamy arm rise from the surf as the woman set out on her journey.

Sixteen Days in December

My father owned every single book P. G. Wodehouse ever wrote. From *Aunts Aren't Gentlemen* through *Carry on, Jeeves* to *Pigs Have Wings* and *Sunset at Blandings*; all the way to *Ukridge*—the titles lined the shelves in his study in alphabetical order. They were about the only things he cared to organize in his life.

"Kala, come here," my father would shout sometimes when he saw me passing by the door of his study. I would go in already knowing what he wanted of me.

"Listen to this," he'd begin. "She 'opened a colored Japanese umbrella in the animal's face. Upon which, it did three back somersaults and retired into private life.' " He would hold up the book with its orange Penguin spine bright under the lamp, his glasses forgotten beside him. " 'Retired into private life.' A dog! 'Retired,' he says!" He would laugh so hard, his eyes streaming, that he could hardly get the sentences out. Often my brother Raj would come in too and we would laugh together, not so much at the old-fashioned comedy but at my father's loud, whooping delight in the words.

The public figure my father admired most was Judge Krishnamurthy of the Indian High Court. Apparently the man opted to write his closing arguments in Wodehousian. When I was ten, I would sit quietly in the corner and watch my father tell the story to his audience, usually young subeditors from his newspaper who had dropped by to pay homage. The renowned judge in his closings would call the plaintiff "a jolly good egg" or proclaim that the defendant was "an old crumpet." As his disciples laughed I would feel pleased that my father was the only one who knew where these strange English phrases that compared people to food came from.

After the first few TIAs (we had become adept at the medical jargon by then) my father couldn't concentrate very well. I would come in sometimes to find him flipping frantically through the pages of his Wodehouse of the week, searching for the part of the story he had left off reading minutes ago. One night he held the book out to me.

"I can't remember. Where did I stop? Can you show me where I stopped?" he said, his pretenses ended, his face pleading and unashamed.

I searched through the book, found a page and pointed to a paragraph. "Here Daddy, here it is, this is exactly where you stopped. See, right here."

My mother forbade me from becoming a journalist like him. She didn't think it was appropriate for a young woman to work night shifts. This was India after all. So what if it was the eighties? No one will want to marry you, she warned. I knew there were other things she held against the profession. Things she never said.

Like the time when I was eleven years old and my father took me to the dentist. The doctor bent over me, pulled out a rotten blue tooth, and laid it in a metal basin. Then he shoved the basin under my chin with a grand flourish, expecting me to be as pleased as he was at his handiwork. But all I could do was spit mouthfuls of blood over the tooth, desperate to drown this source of my stupid, uncontrollable tears.

The moment the dentist had poised his instruments over my mouth, my father had gone pale and retreated to the waiting room. They had a radio playing there. Now he came bounding back in, his face shining with excitement.

"The Army's just been called out in UP. Hindu-Muslim riots, shoot-at-sight order, hundreds killed. The whole damn thing just blew up. Are you done, Doc?"

"Sir, you can't smoke in here," the doctor said.

My father sent me home alone in a taxi, my blood-stained handkerchief pressed to my swollen cheek. This was breaking news. He had to get to work. I was to tell my mother. He didn't know when he'd be home. He and the taxi driver discussed politics all the way to the newspaper office.

"A Communist takeover, that's what this country needs," my father said. It was something I'd heard him say many times before. I imagined soldiers in fur coats and hats like those in the movie *Doctor Zhivago* marching through our streets. My father forgot to give the driver directions to our house as he jumped out and the man had to yell after him to ask. I didn't protest. I was still recovering from the sight of all that blood.

When I got home my mother was furious. I could tell from the way she held her mouth. "Your father had to go. It's his work—the newspaper has to come out at a certain time every day. And this is big news which has to be in the paper."

Later I heard her talking to her friend Chandini next door when she thought I was asleep. No one sent young girls home alone in taxis with strange men. Was the man mad? One heard such stories. What does one do with such a man?

"Did the Army catch them?" I asked my father when he came home the next afternoon.

"Who?" He looked tired in his day-old shirt. Now he handed me *The Last Term at Malory Towers* by Enid Blyton. He had stopped at the library on his way home.

I was addicted to the stories and fantasized about being sent away to a boarding school exactly like the British one. But now I barely looked at it.

"The people who did it." I had woken early to wait for the newspaper wallah. I had seen the pictures before anyone else in the house. The rows of filled hospital beds. The men agape around the burning bus. The black-veiled women squatting beside their wounded children like huge sad crows.

My father looked over at my mother before he answered. When I showed her the newspaper my mother asked why they had to put such shots on the front page.

"No. The Army didn't catch them, Kala." He rubbed his knuckles across his temple. "They would have to arrest entire villages, every single able-bodied male in some of those towns. Do you understand?"

I didn't. I was about to ask him to explain but he looked so angry, so unlike my usual easygoing father, that I merely nodded.

My mother liked to say that the house we lived in was the only thing of lasting value he'd bought her. If he overheard her, he'd reply, "Who asked you to marry a journalist?" She'd said she wanted neighbors, other women she could talk to nearby, and my father had found her this house.

It was small with big windows that looked out onto tall tamarind and neem trees. There were five other houses just like ours. They all had front doors and porches that opened into the same large courtyard. In the summer the women used the open space to dry chillies and cure pickles in large glass jars and the men read the newspaper in their vests in the evenings and argued about politics until it grew too dark to see and their wives called them in to dinner.

My father, home from his after-work trip to the bar, would stop and talk with the men, swaying a little, his words blurring as he repeated the same sentences over and over again. The other men would pretend that he was one of them, clean-living, middle-class family men who came home straight from work at 5:30, with cloth bags of fresh vegetables swinging from their hands. I would watch from my room, my stomach churning, wishing he would come in, away from their polite, knowing faces.

A low stone wall ran around the houses and there was only one gate to get in. The wall and the gate created a feeling of being in a calm, private space, separate from the city outside. It brought the people who lived here together.

But Raj and I had stopped sitting on our porch steps with the other kids. We didn't want to be the ones to answer curious questions about my father or why I wasn't married yet. That was my mother's job. Although the questions had stopped after he had the stroke.

One Sunday morning in 1988, a few weeks after I had started in my first job as a journalist for a woman's magazine, my father woke up, sleepy still after watching World Cup football till 2 a.m., reached for the coffee cup beside him, and had a seizure. He fell off the bed and lay shivering, saliva pouring out of his mouth, while mother and I stood over him panic-stricken, still chewing our breakfast. He was fifty-two years old. Obviously, the pills they had given him for his TIAs didn't work very well.

After we brought him back from the hospital my brother Raj and I weren't allowed to enter his room. "Gesh oush, bashtars," he'd yell when he saw us hovering by the door. He flung a framed photo of the four of us on vacation at Raj's head the day he tried to sneak in. It was a powerful throw for a man who had only one workable side. But nothing he did stopped my mother.

One afternoon I stood outside the door and watched her, twelve years younger than he, comb her hair beside my father's bed, her face intent on wresting meaning out of the distorted sounds that gurgled from his mouth. Under her absent-minded brushing, her hair was black and vital, crackling with static energy. To me it seemed as if her womanliness was mocking the man in front of her.

Abruptly, he stopped protesting when he saw us. The day we were finally allowed inside, Raj and I sat with him for hours. Raj read to him from *Pigs Have Wings,* sounding jolly. My father didn't even open his eyes. I couldn't think of one thing to say. After we came out of the room Raj and I went into my room and closed the door. He held me as I cried, very quietly so my mother wouldn't hear.

A week later she called me at work.

"There's dal and rice on the ceiling. He kicked me and the lunch plate went flying across the room." She laughed the nervous, amazed laugh she had acquired recently. It was as if she could do nothing but marvel at what had become of her husband.

"Are you all right, Mom?"

"Yes. Yes. What could be wrong with me? I'll be okay once I lie down." That laugh again. "What will I do if he refuses to eat like this?"

My mother got up a dozen times at night to check on him; dragged the unyielding, dead weight of his body to the toilet. He wouldn't let anyone else do it. Once she turned from her image in the mirror and said to me, as if noting an interesting fact about someone else, "I am back to the size I was fifteen years ago. I could probably fit into your blouses."

Most of the time my father lay there mute, stricken, reduced to swatting sullenly at the spoons that were raised to his mouth and then staring at the flopping anarchy of his hand.

Other times there were what my mother delicately called "episodes." He kicked over a small side table crowded with his medicines. I watched his left foot tap furiously side to side like a metronome while I mopped up the mess of broken bottles and strong-smelling liquids on the floor. After that we kept every breakable thing out of his reach.

Over her screams, he pulled at a handful of my mother's hair until it nearly came off her scalp. Raj and I didn't find out until we came home from work.

"This can't go on—he might kill her. Something has to be done," Chandini whispered, dragging me into her dark, cluttered living room. I wanted to tell her that she hadn't seen how he turned his head to follow my mother as she fussed around his room.

Still, I tried talking to him. He stared out of the window as if I weren't even there.

"Don't take that tone with your father. He doesn't know what he's doing. I know he doesn't," my mother said.

The Hindu-Muslim riots that broke out in North India brought him back to us. It seems obvious now. Anyone could have made the connection that a former journalist would be interested in the news. Somehow we didn't think of it until I saw my father listening intently to the radio's faint mutterings in the living room. Those first few months we were all too busy just coping.

We moved the Sony radio that Raj had bought with his first paycheck into his room the day general elections were declared. As I fiddled with it I watched my father's face. When the dial swept past the music stations he closed his eyes. When it caught a newsreader gravely intoning the news he opened them. We kept the radio permanently tuned to the news station. He listened to everything—even the agricultural news for farmers at 5 p.m.

In the buildup to the elections, Hindu fundamentalist parties had mounted an unsuccessful campaign to demolish a 500-year-old mosque called the Babri Masjid in Ayodhya. They claimed that it stood on the site of a sacred Hindu temple, where according to legend, Rama, the divine hero of the epic *Ramayana,* was born. Hindu-Muslim violence broke out and over 800 people were killed in North India. The first time the announcer came on to tell us the number of the dead, my father whispered "bashtar polishes," over and over again. They were the first words he had said in weeks. He'd always professed a great disdain for politicians.

In the months that followed, V.P. Singh became Prime Minister and somehow managed to foil Hindu fundamentalist schemes to destroy the mosque. The country held its breath as one crisis slid inexorably into the next. My father had begun to sit propped up with pillows, and sometimes even made an attempt to turn the pages of the newspaper with his left hand. My mother had taken to leaving a pad and pencil on the night table next to him. She said she saw his fingers making scribbling motions as he listened to the radio.

Then one blustery day in November the government fell and my father began an editorial.

"He's been writing something these last few days," Mother whispered to me one day when I came home from work. She looked excited. "Don't ask him, you know how he gets."

A few days later I picked up the paper and went into his room to read to him. My father was sitting up, listing to the right as always. He had the pad on his lap.

When he saw me, he jogged the pad slightly. "Kala," he said.

"Do you want me to read it?" I asked him. When I was younger, I had a scrapbook into which I pasted everything he wrote, carefully scissoring around his articles in the paper. I used to turn to the op-ed page and be freshly astonished that someone I saw every day could have his name printed atop a special framed column for the world to see.

He nodded. "Edit," he said.

I took the pad from him. The sentences that followed were scrawled on the page with great effort, gouging the paper here and there. The letters straggled and wavered like those of a child learning to write. But I could still decipher them.

The recent violence in North India should be taken as a warning of things to come. V.P. Singh, in his wisdom has seen fit to evoke the law of the land to quell the irresponsible rhetoric of the rival factions. He is a jolly good egg. He is trying, dammit. Bastards all politicians. Shhhh. Too much noise. All quiet on the western front. The children are playing. This is All India Radio. The news. This is All India Radio. The news. The news. Read by Ranjit Rathod.

After that there were marks on the page that looped and whorled, not forming any recognizable letters. There were squiggles and wayward lines, a few neatly spaced out like sentences, ending in careful periods. I flipped through the pages. There were five, each one filled with incomprehensible scribbles.

I looked up at my father. I wasn't going to lie to him. I would not do him that indignity. He watched me lean over and put the pad back on his table. Beady-eyed. Sternly awaiting my verdict. Perhaps there was a well-argued analysis of the current political situation in his head. Perhaps everything made perfect sense to him.

"Shall we read the pap—" I began, and my voice broke. I was doing what I had promised myself I would never do in front of him. Crying.

"Shhh. Shhh," he said, suddenly turned into an old, sick man with disheveled hair and eyes that still understood.

When I said goodbye to my father months later he looked at me, his eyes blank above his awry mouth, for a long time. Then he turned his head away and closed his eyes. There was a thin strand of saliva spooling sideways out of the corner of his mouth and I took the towel my mother hung on the headboard and wiped it off. I explained it all to him—my transfer to the Bangalore office of the magazine, my new position which would let me send more money home to pay the medical bills, the new car I was getting—laying the words out like offerings. All he did was stare curiously at my lips as if he could see strange objects emerging from my throat. I didn't know what, if anything, he could comprehend anymore. He hadn't said a single word in over a year. The doctors suspected the paralysis was spreading.

Eight months later my mother's telegram simply read, "Father sick. Start immediately." I hadn't been home since I'd begun the new job in Bangalore. I'd convinced myself I was too busy.

The matronly sales representative behind the counter at Jet

Airways would not find me a seat even after I showed her the telegram.

"If the telegram said 'father dead' we could have done something. But with the Ayodhya thing, there are a lot of people trying to get home," she whispered.

The conflict over the mosque in Ayodhya had flared up again. The rhetoric had grown uglier in these last few weeks. In the past few days, thousands of Hindu youth had been gathering in Ayodhya, and rumors spread of potential violence and rioting. Scared families were hurrying to be together. I tried calling home but the phone was dead.

The train was six hours late and by the time we got to Hyderabad the city was under curfew. I rode home in a taxi with a police jeep following, its siren at full throttle. The telegram worked this time.

"Masjid ko thod diya," said the driver, a young Muslim man with kohl smudged black around his eyes. He slowed the taxi to spit a long stream of tobacco juice with contemptuous force onto the road, and wiped his mouth with the scarf around his neck. They had demolished the mosque. I saw him watching me in the narrow mirror fixed above the windshield.

"I need to get home quickly, my father is very sick," I confided to this stranger. He didn't say a word after that, neither did he drive any faster.

It was only afterward, when I saw the frenzied, ecstatic Hindu men on TV swarming over the ancient weathered dome of the Babri Masjid mosque, prying the bricks out one by one to throw down to the bellowing crowds, that I thought about him, a Muslim driving me home without demur.

I asked the driver to stop at the mouth of the long dirt lane that led to my house. The police jeep idled behind us, its mournful siren announcing my arrival.

When I walked in through the gate the children and women standing quietly outside moved away. Someone took my suitcase. Daddy must be very sick to have gathered such a crowd, I thought.

In the bedroom my mother lay on her bed resting, surrounded by her sisters and friends. She felt small and unfamiliar in my arms, her damp face pressed into my neck like a tired child's. Why wasn't she in hospital with my father? I wondered.

"I did everything I could, didn't I? I was with him until the last minute, wasn't I?" she said as if I was accusing her. Only then I realized that my father was dead.

"They took him away two hours ago," said my aunt Vani. "They could not wait anymore. The priests wouldn't allow it." Aunt Vani had the same high forehead and square jaw that my mother and I shared. Everyone remarked on the family resemblance.

"But the telegram? What about the telegram?" I let go of my mother and fumbled in my purse.

"She didn't want you to panic. She thought you'd fly anyway." Aunt Vani put her arms around my shoulders. I was twenty-six, yet Mother felt the need to shield me from life, to tell me her lies.

"The train was six hours late . . . there were no flights . . . this Ayodhya thing. People were coming back to their families," I said. It seemed important to give explanations.

"Maybe it is best you didn't see the body. He was so thin, like a skeleton in the end," another of the women said, her eyes red from crying.

With us death is not a private affair. I was different, alien, in not knowing how to wail in front of everyone else.

My mother moved away from me to lie down again, turning her back to the women in the room—the neighbor ladies, as

Raj and I called them. "You musn't cry. He doesn't have to suffer anymore. Think of him as you last saw him," she mur-
mured into the wall, already returned to her grief.

Hours later I forced myself to step into my father's study.
They'd told me my father had been laid out here before he
was taken away. The walls of the room were lined with the
books my father had bought in railway stations, sidewalk stands,
musty shops.

An old man I had never seen before, probably somebody's
grandfather on a visit, was dozing in my father's armchair. I
stood in the doorway and watched him breathe, his slight chest
hardly moving. When I walked in the old man awoke with a
snort and stared at me with unfocused eyes.

"You're the daughter? Did you just get here?" he asked me
as if he had been expecting me. As he shuffled out he reached
up and patted me distractedly on the head.

My father's old rolltop desk was pulled slightly out of its
customary place in the middle of the room, blocking my view
of the rest of the floor. There was a faint smell of incense. The
room looked disheveled and unfamiliar. The chairs had been
pushed up against the wall and the threadbare carpet rolled up
and propped in a corner.

I slipped around the desk and stopped, drawing my foot
back. I was hesitating at the edge of the space where a few
hours ago they had laid my father's body down. The vessels
used for the last rites gleamed dully on the floor, reflecting the
diffused light of early evening that came in through the drawn
curtains. There were empty brass pots and large plates bare except for a few leftover strands of holy Darba grass. There were
bowls for oil and urns of rice, depleted now, the grains spilled
and scattered. Tangled lengths of white muslin lay where they
had been thrown beside incense stands with circles of ash at

their base, and petals had fallen here and there, their edges already dry and curled. Here was all the debris of ritual abandoned in the flurry of departure. The ragged careless arrangement had marked the boundary around my father's body. Now the line of clutter only traced vacant space, outlining the emptiness and absence contained in that small patch of perfectly ordinary mosaic floor.

In the hours I sat with her my mother recounted his last moments over and over again, the dinner she had fed him, the hiccups he'd had, the holy Ganga water she had had the presence of mind to pour into his mouth. In the end he looked serene, she said.

My father had been three inches shorter than I. We had measured it one day, long after I had stopped growing. The pencil marks were still there on the wall beside his desk. I carefully moved the lamp with the blackened wicks that must have stayed lit at his feet and knelt down to lay my palms on the empty floor where my father had been. Then I got to my feet and stepped over the vessels, lay down in the center, and stretched myself out.

Afterward Raj said that the most difficult thing of all was searching for my father's tooth.

"It's considered auspicious for the son to find it," he explained with his newfound knowledge of funeral rites.

Immediately I imagined the tips of my fingers scrabbling in the ash, shifting sharp-edged bones aside, searching for a tooth-like shape. Did teeth separate from the gums they were fixed in, drift apart in the heat somehow?

"Uncle Mohan and the rest of the men were gathering bones like twigs, shoving bits and pieces into the urns anyhow.

I just watched, I didn't know what to do." Raj's hair was mashed down sideways after his nap. He had wandered into my bedroom, his face still puffy with sleep. "Pretty barbaric to make the son light his father's pyre . . . make him watch," he said. Even now, seven days after the cremation, his voice trembled slightly. He cleared his throat.

When he'd come back from the funeral ghats at 3 a.m. there had been a streak of soot high above his left eye. It seemed so long ago.

"Did you dream of it just now?" I put aside my book.

"No," he said, walking toward the door and rubbing his new beard. He wasn't allowed to shave until the sixteenth day. We hadn't really talked until now. The house had been full of people and mother had needed attention. "Would you like some tea?" Raj asked from the dining room.

"There isn't any, I think. We've run out of almost everything. Maybe you should go and buy a few things when they lift the curfew tonight." I raised my voice and then remembered that mother was asleep.

The local news channel had announced that the curfew would be lifted at 5:00 p.m. for two hours. The camera lingered on the bored soldiers standing guard over wooden carts of tomatoes and onions at the Nampally Market. For once, they were showing us how things were here, in Hyderabad, instead of far away in Bombay or Delhi. The voice-over said the government was making every effort to see that people could go on with their daily lives, while the camera panned over a deserted railway platform where stray dogs roamed with impunity. Someone at the TV station had evidently goofed up on the editing.

Raj came back and sat down with a cup in his hand.

"Aunt Vani says Mother is asleep," he said. "She is eating at last, ate some lunch." He stared ahead, the fingers of his other hand drumming restlessly on his knee, his eyes shifting rapidly between my face and the asoka trees with their drooping leaves outside the window.

On the day my father died the neighbors had sent tea, food, and chairs for the visitors. They had helped Raj make the phone calls to our relatives. Even with the curfew our uncles and aunts had managed to come. The methods they had used to get here, the policemen they had to bribe, the local politicos they had to call, started the conversation and kept it going with every new arrival. Ayodhya was never far from anyone's mind.

Sitting alone in the quiet living room in the hours after my arrival, I had heard them, the neighbors and my uncles, arguing in the courtyard.

"The government should have stopped it—they knew the Vishwa Hindu Parishad was going to tear it down. They should have known there would be hell to pay," someone started.

"It's ridiculous, did these people suddenly discover it was Lord Rama's birthplace? The mosque has stood there for centuries, for God's sake." Mr. Jaganathan's thick, Tamil-accented English was unmistakable.

"It is time these Muslims were taught a lesson—after all, this is a Hindu country." That would be Mr. Krishnan, the vicious conservative. There was a general chorus of agreement.

I had wanted to go out there and scream at them, How dare you, how dare you. My father would have thrown them out of the house. But my mother would have been shocked and ashamed; one didn't make scenes in a house of death. So I stood panting a little in the middle of the room, wishing for I don't know what . . . for an end to all this talk, for silence.

Raj said, "I shouted at Mother that day. She threw herself on Daddy when I was lifting him to take him away . . . Her hair got stuck in my watch strap. I had to drag her away." Raj had shouted Stop it, stop it, and she had turned her red, streaming face to him like a stranger who turns to you when you say excuse me behind her on a bus. Was that how it had happened? Poor Raj. He had done it all alone.

"Raj, why didn't you wait for me?" I asked. My brother sat at the foot of my bed quietly, not even demanding conversation of me. He had always willingly played the younger sibling, asking my advice on everything—his jobs, his clothes, his women.

"It's these damn uncles, and the priests. They just took over. Anyway, there's nothing you could have done. Women aren't allowed at cremations, you know that," he said quickly, as if he had rehearsed the sentence. It was true, there was nothing I could have done.

"Mother wanted—" he began.

"I think I'll watch some TV," I said and left the room. I did not want to talk to Raj anymore. I did not want him to drag out the bits and pieces inside him for my inspection and forgiveness.

I switched on the BBC. Only the foreign correspondents on its programs seemed to have the right figures for those killed once the riots started, in the first few hours after the mosque was destroyed. On the Indian national news the anchors came on and read us the untruth of the hour in suitably somber tones.

"The situation is tense but under control," they said, over and over again.

Now the British newscaster counted off numbers like an accountant. Thousands had been killed in Bombay, both Muslims and Hindus. Antioc Hill, Crawford Market—the familiar names were now markers for sites where the worst massacres had occurred.

On TV there were no people in the streets, but even the Army could not control the crowds at the hospitals. The corpses had overflowed out of the morgues into the courtyards and parking lots. Hovering at a discreet distance, the camera showed row upon row of elongated white shapes on the ground. They could have been anything—bundles of laundry or pillows. The camera began tracking one young woman. One hand holding the end of her sari to her nose, she walked down the rows, stopping often to lift the corner of a sheet and peer at the uncovered face. She was searching methodically, doggedly, for that one missing dead body that belonged to her. Later, at the end of the news, they showed us the situation in other, smaller towns. In the underequipped district hospitals there were no sheets, and ordinary men and women sifted through bodies mounded in the corridors. A whole nation was trying to find its dead.

After six days of curfew, Raj decided to go out and get groceries. I had misgivings. We had heard from one of the neighbors that people were being stabbed at traffic crossings. Mr. Jaganathan's cousin was on his scooter when he felt a sharp pain and looked down at a lap full of blood—someone with a tiny hidden dagger had sliced straight across his underbelly and sped away when the lights changed.

Raj was late coming back. I imagined him walking in, his fingers gripping his red middle, his guts colorful and slippery in his hands, standing in the doorway with an angry face, upset at how careless he had been.

"They are selling tomatoes at sixty rupees a kilo and people are still buying," he said when he came back, his hands full of packages, the new fanny pack that he had lately started affecting snug round his uninjured waist.

"I hope you didn't buy any," my mother said, restored to her self a little, just enough to sit at the dining table with us now and then. "I am never going to eat meat again," she added, irrelevantly.

Women gave up something when their husbands died. We had persuaded mother not to wear widow's white, but she found it necessary to make some kind of sacrifice. Maybe in another culture, in some faraway country, daughters gave up something too, a favored food or habit that would remind them of their loss every day. It was only fitting that one made some concrete, measurable gesture of grief.

Raj and my mother started talking of how they had bathed my father when he died. They laid him on the veranda in the back of the house and she had bathed him just as she had done every day for four years. Left with nothing but their ever-growing piles of words, I wanted to ask my brother, How did it feel, Raj? Describe exactly how it felt.

Raj had always helped Daddy get changed after he brought him home slack-jawed from one of the bars he frequented. After the first TIAs the doctors had advised him not to drink, drive, or smoke. He'd obeyed them about the driving. Raj would hold my father steady with one arm around his shoulders while he unbuttoned his shirt and drew his belt out of his pants with the other. Sometimes my brother would laugh a little at this grown man lurching in his arms, and Daddy, grateful to be forgiven, would grin eagerly and repeat the same excuse. "A little too much tonight . . . the typesetting boys wanted to take me out."

First it had been his colleagues, then the subeditors, then peons and typesetters, then finally anyone willing to buy him a drink. My brother had told me yesterday what he'd known for years—Daddy was usually alone when he went to pick him up at the bar.

When the wailing started on the seventh night, Raj blundered into my room, his eyes rolling in panic.

"Mother! Is she all right?" he shouted.

The three of us sat in the bedroom too afraid even to switch on the lights. The cries of terrified women and children beat against the closed windows, so loud and close it was as if they were just a few yards outside the walls of the compound.

"In Allah's name have mercy, don't kill my babies! Have mercy, brothers." With long, sobbing ululations the women cried and pleaded with mysterious killers.

"They are raping our mothers, the Hindu dogs are killing our men! Help us! Help us!" some others shrieked.

When the women's lamentations died down to a despairing murmur for an instant, I heard a baby crying, its repetitive cries rising and falling in the background. Then they started screaming again and its thin voice was lost. It was a terrible sound, this disembodied resonance of death taking place somewhere else, unseen in the dark. Transfixed by this howling complaint against the inexorable advance of loss, I trembled with the need to feel my fists strike back against some attackers, to sink a knife triumphantly into resisting flesh.

Raj sat between us on the bed with his arms around our shoulders. I could feel his heart thumping against my side. He did the right thing so easily, without any self-consciousness. He kept saying shhh, shhh, as if to quiet not just us but also the women outside. I wanted to be alone inside some thick darkness, with nothing but the comforting silence of insensate, animal things quietly scrabbling in the mud somewhere nearby.

After what seemed like hours, the wails stopped abruptly and we heard sirens in the distance. Mother couldn't sleep and

I listened to her and Raj murmuring together in her room until dawn.

In the morning, the police inspector in charge of our precinct held a meeting with the men inside the compound. The sounds we'd heard were recordings blasted from loudspeakers fixed on parked cars. Religious fundamentalists had created the tapes with soundtracks bought from music studios in Bombay. The bootleg tapes were flooding the markets.

"They are being used by unscrupulous elements to incite Muslim neighborhoods to violence. Whole Hindu neighborhoods are being wiped out in response. But we are doing our best to control this menace," the inspector reassured us, as if he was quoting from a report, his mouth prissy under his neat mustache.

"The Hindus are doing the same thing," he said, except they had the women on the tapes calling upon Rama and Krishna to save them. Then the inspector squared his cap and left.

So it was just smart technology, mere mimicry of terror. We had been taken in. I thought of my mother's broken breathy prayers and my dread last night in the dark bedroom. Only the effects of their game were real—sleeping men and women dragged out of their tangled beds and run through with daggers and kitchen knives.

Later that day Aunt Vani dropped by to ask me to help her air out Daddy's clothes—the shirts and pants he hadn't worn in years because he had never gone anywhere except to the hospital a couple of times—before she gave them away. We hung the clothes on the line out back, and I watched the shirts on their hangers in the sunlight, arms and torsos fluttering and billowing, now full and round, now empty, filled with nothing but the breeze. In the evening when we brought them in they had no scent, except that of having been in the sun, and I could no longer remember which were the ones I had seen Daddy wear.

When daytime curfew was lifted my mother said it was a miracle. "It's as if Lord Krishna knew that we had to perform the Sixteenth Day Ceremony," she told my uncle in the car two days later. We were on our way to Vijaywada with the last two earthen urns that had been set aside for this day. With the ashes consigned to the confluence of two rivers, the period of mourning would be officially over, Raj could shave, I could leave and go back to my job.

On the steps of the embankment leading down to the river, the thin, bare-chested priest sat cross-legged in front of us, his wet clothes plastered to his boyish hips. He was shivering slightly from his dip in the river. Amid the restless crowds who clambered up and down the steps, the three of us sat in a quiet huddle facing the priest. He untied the cloths bound tightly across the mouth of the urns and tipped their contents, a few small fragments of charred bones and ash, onto the green banana leaf in front of me. I, who had never seen a dead body in my life, was finally performing the only funeral rite I was allowed.

While the priest chanted his prayers, I held the bones in my hands and waited for something to happen—for the familiar father scent of tobacco and rum to permeate me, or for their brittle, pitted surfaces to transmit some forgotten but precious memory. The bones remained remote, devoid of magic or power, unfamiliar as driftwood. Finally I let them fall back onto the leaf and the priest threw everything into the water. The bones sank immediately and left only gray dust and a few white petals floating on the waves to show where they had been. Climbing back up the steps, threading carefully between the chattering women changing out of their soaking saris after their bath and children shrieking at stray dogs, I thought of the ashes and bones settling eventually into the ancient mud at the bottom of the river.

When we got back it was Sunday and there was a group of men in the far corner of the courtyard. It was fresh and cool and in the blue sunlit haze of the morning the only sound was the dry scrape of leaves on the ground. The circle of men rippled apart quietly to accommodate our intrusion and then closed again. They stood silent and riveted, feet in flip-flops and unbuckled sandals, arranged in a wide circle as if they were stopped at the edge of some invisible, impassable boundary. And in the middle of that circle on the bare concrete lay the body of the laborer whom our neighbor, Mr. Rao, had hired to lay bricks for the new study he was adding to his house. We had seen the thin man around now and then, sitting under the trees with his mousy wife eating his midday meal. He had managed to come to work even during the curfew. His wife had gone looking for him when he didn't come back at night and found him where his killers had left him, a few yards away from our gate. She sat beside him saying nothing but raising her arms upward now and then, as if wordlessly pleading for answers.

The small man lay in the courtyard stretched out neatly, his arms held a little away from his body as if he had been about to flap them when the dagger found him. His narrow gray head sat on a neck and shoulders that were gnarled and stringy, the tendons and muscles over the bones visible clearly under his skin. His was a body of hollows, and even in the bright sunlight there were shadows in the deep dips of his collarbone, in the depression below his prominent Adam's apple, and in the concave top of his belly. His wife had laid a cloth around his middle to cover his wounded, opened stomach and his thighs. From under the dirty, yellowed fabric his legs and the grimy soles of his feet splayed out. His face looked calm, untouched by pain or terror, as if he had turned to his killers and raised a serene hand in greeting, stood there calmly while they drew the vertical slash on his body. Here it was then—the body. Mutilated, yet a locus where you could say here was where it happened. Here was unalterable proof of conclusion situated and concentrated, made visible in the narrow chest and furred ears of this stranger lying in the sunlight with his face turned up to us.

Raj came and raised me from among the men's feet where I had knelt when I could not stand anymore, and walked me home. I leaned on him and then I slept. Later when I was better he told me that the police had come and taken the body away; they would conduct an investigation into the matter. I looked for the wife of the dead man with a vague idea of helping her somehow, but no one knew where she had gone.

A few days after that, we locked up the house and left for Bangalore, all of us together. I had decided my mother needed a change. Walking out of the courtyard with Raj and Mother I looked back at the place where the man had lain. It looked familiar and unremarkable, just rough concrete under the flickering shadows of leaves.

Summer

When the bus, which has imprisoned her for three hours inside its rattle and wheeze, finally stops at the big tree that serves as the only bus stop for the entire village, Rani jumps off its last step and starts running. The unsmiling uncle who is glad to hand her over to her parents for the summer stumbles off the bus behind her. "Wait, you stupid girl, wait!" he shouts.

She looks back at him lumbering after her with her heavy suitcase. She will be out of his hands in a few minutes. Then she will be free of his rages and his cold gray house for the summer months. She does not stop. When she gets to the edge of the dirt road, green rice paddies spread out before her like a lake. The sunlight touches everything with blue and gold. She dives in. The bright fields smell of cow dung and mud drying slowly in the sun. It is a smell she forgets in noisy classrooms in town. Now, as always, it surprises her.

She runs with a happy, headlong rush, her arms out-stretched. Her frayed school satchel, filled with vacation home-work she will finish before the cousins arrive, bounces on her thin behind and her long doubled plaits swing heavily below her shoulders. A kingfisher, blue wings flashing, skims and swoops ahead of her over the slender curb of hard-packed mud that follows the line of the fields. It is late April in the year 1957 and Rani is eleven years old.

She arrives panting at the narrow iron gate at the back of the house. It does not open at first and she panics. What if they—father, mother, grandparents, baby sister—have all gone away and left her? It's like a dream she has sometimes. In the dream the sun shines brightly into the empty rooms of her grandfather's house. She looks into the mirrors, which hang beside the beds, but she cannot see herself. When she pushes harder at the gate it opens and she rushes through into the leaf-strewn garden shouting for her mother and grandmother.

"Amma! Amamma! I am home."

Nobody looks any different and Rani is glad. She worries about things like that. Her baby sister on her mother's hip is rounder but she is still a baby. Inside her mouth, Rani feels the serrated edge of a new tooth. Her grandmother still smells of camphor and incense from her prayer room. Her father calls her puppy dog, snub nose, sputnik, tortoise—everything but her name. As always. Rani has been away at school for seven months. Her parents had told her over and over again, gently and patiently, that only the town school could teach her to speak English as fluently as her cousins from the city did. Then they had returned to the village and left her alone. Now she runs around her grandfather's house, climbs up and down the wooden stairs, peers into the bedrooms, and claims its spaces all over again. In Rani's mind it is always summer here—even when the pale purple rain beats against the roofs of her uncle's house in town.

The next day Rani visits the fields and pushes her palm into wet ground between the neat rows of rice plants. The mud spurts up in thick brown ropes between her fingers. How angry her uncle would be if he could see her now. But he has returned to his big house in the town. She respectfully bent down and touched his feet in farewell, following her mother's whispered instructions. She looks at an earthworm wriggling itself loose from the mud near her hand and snatches her hand away. She stands by the pond beside the field and watches catfish flicker and wink in its depths. She breathes in the mossy green smell and feels full and content.

Rani can hardly wait for her cousins to arrive. Her mother catches her looking at the clock and teases her. "The cousins. They are all you think about. Maybe they won't come this year. Maybe they forgot."

The cousins don't forget. They arrive in batches, all eleven of them. They come from Bombay, Poona, Bangalore, Kanpur, Baroda, from cities hundreds, thousands of miles away, cities she has only heard of and never seen. They come with their parents, her aunts and uncles, and bring storybooks and fast toy cars and words in strange languages. When the last four step off the bus the others clap and cheer. Rani thinks of the few movies she has seen and the crowd cheering when the villain lies defeated at the hero's feet. She walks back to the house surrounded by a noisy, milling, fighting carnival of brothers. She hugs herself as if to keep her happiness from spilling out.

Ravi is six and wears glasses so thick his eyes look as if they float under water. The others call him Coca-Cola but she does not know why. Satish and Suresh are identical twins who refuse to wear the identical shirts their mother, fat Aunt Radha, sews for them on her Singer sewing machine. Of Uncle Bala's five boys, Rani likes Jayan because he taught her to make a boat out of coconut leaves last summer. Vijay sits high up in the branches of his favorite mango tree and reads, peering down dreamily from time to time at the rest of them tumbling about in the leaves. Mohan is the oldest. He is fifteen and wears long pants. He has pale green hair above his upper lip. The other boys think he's a hero. Rani hasn't seen him for the last three summers. She is forbidden to call him by his name and instead has to be respectful and call him Elder Brother. Hari is four years old and is therefore ignored.

Rani is at the center of it all—their only cousin sister and the only girl. But that does not stop her from competing with them—especially Elder Brother. Her grandfather sets aside a mango tree for the cousins to practice their aim. Rani downs two tart green fruits, one after the other. In the evening when their work is done, the farmhands make swings from ropes and planks and hang them from the tallest trees. She watches Mohan stand up on the plank and learns. She bends her knees and pushes forward with her body exactly as he does. Her baggy, flowered dress flattens against her chest and bony, boyish knees, as she, in time with Mohan's powerful sweep beside her, swings in great arcs, higher and higher, until she beats him. For a few seconds she is above him, hanging in the sky almost parallel to the ground. Her mother, passing by, shrieks.

"Stop, stop! Rani, stop! Get off at once. You are a girl, a girl do you hear?"

Her legs tremble when she gets off the swing but she sits down quickly before anyone, especially Mohan, notices.

Rani is with the cousins in the attic when Mohan finds the scratched, black trunk. Inside there are black coats and hats in different shapes. There are long-sleeved white silk shirts with stiff ruffles down their fronts, dressing gowns with Chinese embroidery, belts, sashes, and suspenders. There are other clothes they cannot even identify except to say they are Western. The commotion brings her mother and aunts upstairs.

"Your great-grandfather worked in Burma—for the British. He was a big officer." Her mother picks up a shirt and holds it against herself.

Rani thinks of the two grass-covered mounds in the mango grove. They mark the places where the pyres of her great-grandparents were lit. She was a baby when they died. In the photographs on the walls downstairs Great-grandfather has bushy eyebrows and a broad, serious face. He looks as if he never smiles. One of them shows him standing straight and saluting a flag. She is sure he would have been angry with them for trying on his clothes. The mothers try to grab the hats off their heads. They laugh as the boys stumble across the dusty wooden floors clutching scratchy white wool pants to their waists. Rani's mother chases them through the black-bottomed cooking pots, broken chairs, and pesticide sprayers strewn on the floor of the attic.

"Enough! Enough! Put them back," she says.

Mohan wraps a maroon silk dressing gown around his length and walks with a measured step toward Rani. He flings one end of the gown back with a flourish, draws an imaginary sword, and cuts off her head.

"Let us do a play," he says. "I will be King."

"I will be Queen," Rani says.

"You can't be Queen," says Jayan. "A Queen is the wife of a King. You are his sister."

"It's a play, it's not real."

"What's a *play*, anyway? I can play too. See . . . see I am playing." Jayan runs around the room and makes train noises.

"I am the only girl here. I have to be Queen."

"She is the only girl here." Vijay always takes her side.

"Put those clothes back into the trunk this minute." Rani's mother sneezes from the dust and covers her nose with her sari.

"Ask Elder Brother," Suresh says. "Can she be Queen?"

"I'll be a soldier." Satish snaps red suspenders across his chest.

Rani runs downstairs and tells her grandmother that she is to be Queen.

Rani's father and Vijay write out the parts from the *Ramayana* and hand them to the cousins. The *Ramayana* is their first choice. They have grown up with its heroes, fallen asleep most nights with its stories intoned in their ears by a sleepy parent. The parents tell them it is a tale of right conduct, that Rama, the Righteous Prince, represents the perfect man. But they forget the philosophy and only remember that the Prince snaps an unbreakable bow in two and wins his wife, that he is sent into exile, that there are demons and chariots and celestial battles.

The adults frown when Mohan changes the story line. The jealous wife of the King is changed into a wicked uncle at Rani's urging. Now it is the wicked uncle who demands a boon of the old King and tricks him into banishing his beloved son, the Righteous Prince, into the forest for fourteen years. The younger brother who accompanies the royal couple into the forest in the original story does not exist in the cousins' version. Now only Rani as the Princess is allowed to fall at the feet of the Righteous Prince. Only she is granted the right to follow him into exile. She is the only one he looks at with longing. "Come, my love," he says.

They practice in the evening in the clearing under the

hundred-year-old tree behind the house. It is rumored to have stood there for centuries. In the dusk, it moves above them and sighs like a great animal. They fetch lanterns as it gets darker and stand solemnly at their chalk-marked positions inside the circle of lamplight. There is a part for everyone in the play. The small boys are trees in the forest.

The grown-ups are not allowed to watch even though the aunts take in coats and sew up sleeves. They will see it only on the big day, when the play will be staged for all of them. Rani thinks it's like a real play, just like the one they had at school last December. At night she takes a long time to fall asleep.

In the daytime the children riot around the house, except Vijay. He sits in his mango tree and reads, swaying gently above the ground. His mother says his hunched shoulders come from reading so much. He is twelve, sharp-featured and brown, and he never teases her. His eyes have long lashes, which Rani thinks are just like the white cow's, the one her grandmother milks every morning. If Rani sits down quietly beneath his tree long enough, he will climb down halfway and talk to her.

"This house is an island," Vijay says one morning. "It is one circle inside two other circles."

"So is it an island or a circle?" She has been in the pond, trying to lure fish onto a thin cloth towel spread underwater. The bottom of her dress is sopping wet, filthy. He does not notice.

"Both. It's the same thing. Look." He climbs back up the tree and she follows him. He swings his arm in a circle, pushing his floppy hair out of his eyes with his other hand. "The house is there, right? That is the first circle. Then there's the courtyard around it—that's the second circle. And then outside these two circles, there are the fields surrounding the house. They are the sea." A cuckoo is learning its call by rote somewhere nearby in the dark green depths of the mango trees.

"Isn't the sea blue?" She has never seen the sea. But in her geography textbook it is blue.

"I said the fields are *like* the sea. The house is . . . oh never mind." He turns back to his book.

She peers through the leaves at the rice paddies that begin at the edge of the grove. Beyond the fields, at the far boundary of the property, is the highway that brought them all here. When the summer ends the highway will take them all away.

"Grandfather showed me the stone that marks where our fields end. It's right next to the highway. I'll show it to you if you want."

"I've seen it," he says.

She narrows her eyes to slits and the fields shimmer and melt in the sunlight. She thinks Vijay is very clever. At night, she thinks of all her family around her, sleeping on an island in the middle of the sea.

They get better at remembering their parts. The play is not long. In their version the play has only the Righteous Prince, the dutiful wife, the evil conspiracy, the banishment. Rani gets better at pretending to cry. She falls dramatically at the feet of the young Prince in gratitude when he asks her to go with him to the forest. When he flings off his robe, renouncing his royal status, she bends down and reverently picks it up from the ground. Some evenings after dinner, her father makes her repeat her lines and corrects her pronunciation of the difficult words. "I am sure snub-nosed girls were banned from being Queen," he teases when they are done, and she complains to her mother.

The boys play everything—the uncle, the sages, the King, and the loyal subjects. Grief-stricken by the news of their beloved Prince's imminent exile, they fall to the ground and roll about in the dust lamenting piteously.

There are only ten days left before the big performance. In the afternoon, the house breathes quietly, as if the strong sunlight beating down on its walls absorbs all sound. Even the shouts of the cousins as they run from Rani to hide seem faint and far away. She uncovers her eyes and she is alone in the courtyard. She feels them watching her. They are in the mango grove, behind the lemon trees, under the haystacks, inside the sheds, silently laughing, waiting for her to find them.

She runs on tiptoe, bent over. She enters the mango grove with its soughing trees, and Mohan shoots out an arm from behind the biggest tree and pulls her back against his squatting form. She stumbles into the circle of his outspread legs and bent knees as if she were walking into the arms of her parents, or grandmother. She laughs, excited at having found him so easily.

"You are out, I caught you—I caught you," she says.

"Shhh . . . shhh . . ." he warns and she stops talking, bewildered. Then she can smell the sweat coming off him. For moments she stands obedient and still, subdued by the strangeness of what he is doing to her. She watches a swollen black beetle burrow greedily into the soft bark of a tree in front of her. Half its iridescent carapace sticks out of the trunk like an alien fruit. Mohan shifts his feet among the fallen leaves and the sounds around her—the faint creak of the trees in the wind, a faraway horn, a hen clucking—slam back against her ears, over his breathing. When he does not stop, she twists out of his arms and runs out of the grove into the courtyard and stands panting, her back pressed against the wall of the house. Inside, the adults nap with the doors and windows shuttered against the sun. She cannot take her eyes off the path that leads toward her from the mango grove.

"Cooee, cooee come and get me." The voices of the other cousins come from somewhere, somewhere where they cannot see her. Or him. He walks out of the shadowed grove and his face is frightening, sweaty and hateful. When he saunters past her and the tears come, she runs to the back of the house where no one will see her and ask her questions for which she has no answers.

Rani wets her bed for the first time in years. Her mother thinks it is the excitement of the play. Mohan is everywhere, wherever she is alone. She stays close to the others. She feels safe in the evenings, when they practice the play under the trees. Then she can see him in front of her and she knows he's not somewhere else, waiting. She struggles silently against him and the dry, hurting scrape of his hand, but she doesn't tell anyone. She is afraid of father, mother, grandparents, aunts, and uncles turning away from her, leaving her alone, sending her away. The house becomes full of dark corners. In the mango grove there are too many shadows under the trees.

Rani stops looking at Mohan when she says her lines. She cannot anymore. At night she sleeps in her grandmother's bed. She strokes the spongy, wrinkled flesh of her grandmother's stomach until she falls asleep, as she did when she was four years old.

Sometimes when Rani goes for a bath, she takes off her cotton frock and panties and looks down at herself. She touches her bald, indented shape. "Rani, have you finished?" her mother shouts from outside, and she snatches her hands away and turns on the tap.

She sits with Vijay on the veranda at night. He is easy to sit with. They watch the insects spin drunkenly around the dim bulb strung from the rafters above them.

"People in the old days thought the earth was flat," he says.

"Don't tell lies." She sidles up closer but is careful not to touch him.

"It's in my book, look!" He smells of soap and the coconut oil that gleams in his hair. In the picture the earth looks flat, like a slice of blue-green bread. The straight ledge of the slice hangs suspended over water. There are white waves drawn on the surface of a purple sea.

"People thought that if they walked straight across the earth they would fall off its edge," Vijay says. Far below the flat earth, under the sea, is an animal with a long neck and an armored tail.

"What does that mean?" She tries to read the sentence written next to it in curled, solemn letters.

"It says, here there be monsters. The book says that people drew maps to warn other travelers about creatures waiting to eat them up if they fell off the edge of the world."

A delicious terror runs up her spine. Tentatively, ready to pull her hand back if anything happens, she touches the picture.

The day of the performance finally arrives. The farmhands say they will come with their families to watch the staging. The two Pentecostal nuns who rent the small tiled house at the far end of the property are also invited. The man who mixes the pesticide for spraying the crops says he'll drop by to see what the children are up to. Rani's grandfather orders the farmhands to cut banana trees and lash them to the gateposts. "But there's no festival, why are they cutting the trees?" Jayan asks anyone who will listen to him. In the morning, her mother, chatting all the while with her sisters, oils and combs Rani's long hair. Mohan comes by and banters with the aunts, watching her.

Rani bends her head and shakes her hair. Now it's a curtain and she can no longer see him. By the time her mother ties her hair in a fat cone on top of her head, he's gone.

"He can marry her if he wants to, you know. When she's old enough," Aunt Radha says.

"All those old customs are dying out. Cousins don't marry anymore," says her mother as she rubs fragrant oil into Rani's face. "Stop that." She holds Rani's head when she tries to twist away. "Look how dry your skin is. Are you a boy or a girl?"

"I know, I know. I saw that article in the paper too . . . about how bad it is for the children. It's just that if he decides, he could," Aunt Radha says.

"Oh, we'll see . . . It's all so far away. Who knows what will happen ten years from now?"

"At least you won't have to go looking for a husband for her. Think of all the dowry you'll save." Aunt Radha laughs.

Her mother notices Rani listening and raises her eyebrows. Rani remembers the time when they had a wedding in the house. Aunt Suja and the groom stood facing each other and exchanged garlands of flowers. When Aunt Suja bent to touch her husband's feet, her long gold chain dragged on the ground. Rani had stood with a tray at the gate to welcome the bridegroom home. The lighted lamp on the tray had made her hands hot. She had eaten too much and thrown up afterward. There had been banana trees at the gate, just like today.

Eight o'clock finally arrives and there are over thirty people in the courtyard. Vijay and Rani peer out of the windows and try to count them. The space where the play will be performed is lit up with kerosene lanterns placed along the wall. Earlier in the day, she helped one of the aunts carefully polish the glass globes that enclose the wicks. It was hard to pull each fresh white wick through the metal slit above the hollow that holds the kerosene. People walking behind the red saris the aunts have hung up for curtains on clotheslines throw shadows onto the fabric. Someone raises his hand and Rani thinks it looks like a huge claw. The grown-ups, the neighbors, the farmhands, and their children sit on reed mats in the dark beyond the lamplight. Only her grandparents get chairs.

Vijay bangs on a stainless steel dinner plate with a ladle to announce the start of the play. It begins well. No one forgets any lines. The jealous uncle demands that the old King keep his forgotten promise. The heartbroken King orders the Prince into exile on the very day of his coronation. Satish, as the uncle, rubs his hands and laughs evilly when his plan is realized. The subjects wail and roll on the ground. Somebody in the audience laughs and is shushed. The young Prince is brave, determined.

"I am resolved to obey my father's command, for such is the way of the good. I will go to the forest gladly," he says.

The small boys shake the branches they are carrying and the forest beckons. Rani, the Princess, waits in the garden. She cries when he refuses to take her with him at first.

"I will go to the trackless forest teeming with wild animals and live there as if in my father's house, clinging to your feet alone. My heart is so attached to you that were we to be parted I am resolved to die," she says.

When he finally agrees she cries some more. Then, when her scene ends, she disappears behind the curtain and watches the audience. They smile and whisper and point. The parents laugh proudly.

The curtain draws back for the last scene. The court is assembled and the Righteous Prince stands surrounded by his people, his courtiers, and his soldiers. They are all eager to go into the forest with him. "Let us abandon our gardens, our fields and homes, and follow the Prince," they shout, but he makes them stay. He smiles kindly and forgivingly at everyone, secure in his goodness. In a few minutes he will turn to his Princess and Rani will have to run to him and fall at his feet. She stands with her head bowed, waiting at the far end. She can hear whispers from the spectators seated behind her. Somebody's foot touches her ankle as he shifts in his place. His people quieted at last, the Righteous Prince addresses the multitude.

"Only one person in this entire kingdom will go with me into the forest. As long as she lives a woman's one deity and master is her husband. Therefore your Princess will go with me," he proclaims.

"Long live the Prince. Long live the Princess. May she be blessed with a hundred sons," shouts the crowd.

Rani raises her head and Mohan is looking at her. He is tall and majestic and the brown sackcloth he wears in place of the silk dressing gown he had flung aside earlier hangs from his shoulders like wings. He stands straight with his legs apart, the gold paper crown on his head gleaming in the lamplight. He looks powerful and undefeated. She can see his eyes.

"Come, O beloved wife. Let us depart before the day grows gray." He turns to her and holds out his hand.

She looks at his hand. She looks at his long fingers moving. She looks at him and does not move, does not run to him, does not fall at his feet. There is silence in the courtyard. Moments pass.

"Come, O faithful one. Let us leave now," he improvises.

She looks away and she can see her grandmother smiling and nodding encouragingly at her, mouthing go, go to him.

"Rani, his feet, fall at his feet," somebody whispers loudly from behind her. Mohan drops his arm halfway and hurriedly pulls it up again. He takes a step forward and his hands reach out, close to her face now.

"Come," he says and his voice is different, angry.

"No. No, don't touch me, don't touch me," Rani screams.

When she does not stop her mother lurches to her side and gathers her close. Mohan stands frozen in his place, his eyes panicked in his pale face. When Rani is quiet her mother guides her to the edge of the stage and they step out of the lamp-lit circle. Her waiting father lifts her into his arms. Grand-parents, aunts, uncles, and cousins stand up, moving aside to let them through. No one says anything as divided, arrayed on both sides of the path, they watch Rani and her parents walk away slowly into the dark house.

A Warm Welcome to the President, *Insh'Allah!*

That year the Yamuna flooded our village, two babies and one old man died of cholera and the banana crop turned sickly, yet we were delirious with joy. We were about to be rescued from centuries of utter inconsequence by a visit from the most powerful man in the world.

The news spread from the village officer, Ishmail Din, whose mouth flapped like a torn shoe. It was he who told us last year that his head clerk's baby boy was unfortunate enough to be born with no thumbs. We stared open-mouthed as the ancient jeep from the village office rattled up along the dirt road that ran the entire length of the village. It stopped at the Grameen Bank, the post office, and the Independence High School, and then since there was nowhere else to head for but the river, turned around and came back. Whenever the jeep stopped, the village officer hopped out like a rooster and minced importantly in and out of the buildings. Those of us who were lucky enough to be there at the time bringing tea or fried aloor chop for the postmaster's or the bank manager's midmorning snack heard every word his thin reedy voice coughed out. We were very popular in the tea stalls that day. By evening, every-

89

one in the village knew. Even those who were tending the jute crop at the far end of the village heard the news shouted across the fields through cupped hands.

That evening there was a huge crowd around Muhammad Barkhat's color TV. He was the headmaster of the Independence School and didn't mind sharing his set, although we'd heard that his wife grumbled from time to time. Even our wives wanted to be there. When we agreed, they hurried over bhaath that night and left the dirty dishes for later. The women wouldn't come in, but took up positions outside Muhammad's windows and sent our children into the room to tell us to stand aside so they too could see the screen. By the time the national news came on, the room was packed tighter than the bus to town.

When the announcer mentioned Joipura and the President's name in the same breath there were whistles and cheers. The shouts grew louder when we saw the great man himself. Tall and broad-shouldered, he stood in his gray suit and red tie on the lawn of a five-star hotel, towering over the men and women circling around him. His gray hair glittered in the sun and his wide, full-fleshed face was ruddy in the heat. A few of us even threw coins at the TV. It was as if we were at the local cinema and our favorite action hero had just stepped onto the screen.

"Aha! What color the man has—like sweet curds only," someone shouted.

"Look how much he smiles—they all have perfect teeth in America." The man who spoke considered himself an authority on matters foreign. He had an uncle who went away to America in 1954 and did not come back or write ever again.

"His wife has golden hair and is also running for some election. Praise Allah she wins a great victory," Muhammad Barkhat said from his armchair, and there was a chorus of

Insh'Allahs in the room. On the screen, the President bent
down to shake hands with a small boy dressed in a white-and-
gold punjabi suit. He smiled at the child as if he were his own
son and the lines around his eyes bunched together, pushing
his eyes almost shut. Then his picture disappeared and the announcer came back and stayed on, although we booed enthu-
siastically. The President would go to meet the true people of
Bangladeshi soil in Joipura on October 19, she said.

"The government is considering large-scale investment in
Joipura and the Rural Advancement Committee has recommended special fast-track programs . . ." She squeezed the long
bookish words government TV liked to use out of her tiny
mouth, but we had stopped listening. All we could talk about
was that there were only ten nights and nine days to go.

We held a meeting the next evening under the 150-year-old
banyan tree in the center of our village. Ishmail Din tried to
dominate the proceedings from the beginning.

"The deputy secretary to the Minister for Foreign Affairs
himself called me on his direct line from the capital," he said
and paused as if expecting applause.

We searched behind our ears for a bidi to light up and said
nothing.

"I am to show Clinton the Grameen Bank, the Agricultural
Depot and its new seed distribution program, and then he'll
hold a public meeting," he said talking fast.

A few of us gasped. He was calling the President by his
name, just like that. "Who does this upstart think he is? Did he
whisper the great man's name in his ear at his baby-naming
ceremony?" we muttered among ourselves, shocked at his dis-
respectful ways.

"We'll have to put up a grandstand, a podium here. Dhaka

has sanctioned a special amount." Ishmail paused to draw breath and gazed intently at us.

We looked up at the blue sky through the leaves.

"We will do it. We'll show the President Sahib a great welcome."

Muhammad Barkhat suddenly stepped up next to Ishmail Din. "So who would like to help build the stand?" At his question we all cheered and raised our hands as one man. The village officer's face was like thunder as Muhammad picked out eight of us to build the podium where the President would stand to speak to us. The headmaster continued: "The President Sahib shall also visit the school and—"

"That is not scheduled and I have my orders from the capital," Ishmail dismissed the suggestion before Muhammad could finish. A few of us hissed at him.

Muhammad's Independence School served three villages but had no money. Every morning Muhammad's youngest stood on the steps beating a stick on a steel plate—there wasn't even a bell to rouse our children. We felt it was only right that the President should visit the school.

"Leaders all over the planet listen to him. Surely he could find us some money for our school," we said.

"The President will go to school. The President will go to school," a few of us began chanting, and others took it up.

"We'll see . . . the Minister . . . I'll have to phone," Ishmail spluttered. He stumbled to his jeep and left.

"Who do these people think they are? They should be grateful if a peon from the capital decides to come to this shithole—and here they have the President of the greatest country in the world wanting to visit them. Now they want to direct his every move like traffic policemen. Pah!" he said later in his office, frowning down at his lunch. We heard that a piece of roti got stuck in his throat right after he said that and his back had to be thumped to stop his coughing. We thought he should take that as a sign of Allah's displeasure.

Early the next morning Muhammad Barkhat began marching our children through the village to the tunes of the band. The band was made up of doddering old men, many of whom could barely summon up the breath to blow their trumpets, let alone carry the brass instruments and massive drum around. We usually hired them to play popular movie songs at our weddings. Now here they were, striding along at the head of the column of children, the gold braid on their burgundy uniforms shining in the sun. We stopped at the side of the road on our way to work, forgetting the baskets of fish and vegetables on our bicycles and the bamboo that needed cutting, and watched this wonderful sight. The music, so stirring and clear in the quiet morning, swelled in our heads, and the day stretching ahead suddenly became a festival.

Muhammad's plan was to have the children welcome the President's motorcade. He lined up the children in front of the village office to do their exercises. Yunus, the young science teacher, stood in front of them.

"One, two, three. One, two, three," he shouted as he swiveled his arms with great vigor around his body, the children folllowing him. We applauded. Ishmail Din peered out of his office window at the parade, his face twisted up as if he'd bitten into a green tamarind.

"Even Allah isn't working today with all this noise disturbing his heaven—that's for sure," the blasphemer said.

In the days that followed, our wives left their vegetable patches and hen coops and lined the road to watch the children with narrowed eyes.

"It's a great honor to be chosen to parade in front of the

President. Don't you dare faint on that day. The entire village will laugh at you." The children who did pass out in the sun were secretly fed expensive eggs at night to build their strength.

But Ishmail Din wouldn't give Muhammad a straight answer as to whether the President would visit the school or not. When questioned, he mumbled vague problems about getting through to Dhaka or the Minister being busy with the presidential visit.

We cursed the village officer, but Muhammad merely smiled and shifted the wad of tobacco in his mouth.

Those of us who could, read the papers aloud to the others sitting on the wooden benches in the tea stalls. Sometimes the owner gave us a glass or two of free tea just for reading the news. We read that at a state banquet the President wore a striped blue shirt with a white collar and ate chicken korma, lamb biryani, machher jhol, and our famous dish of prawns in yogurt. Then he finished with two bowls of sweet creamy shemai. We felt a warm affection for this man who enjoyed our food so much. The papers said he insisted on going to the Tomb of the Martyrs to pay homage to the soldiers who had died in the war against Pakistan.

"It is as if we know this great man intimately now," one of us said, expressing the feeling that was growing in us—especially since we saw him on TV every night and in the newspapers every morning. Our children cut his pictures out of the paper and pasted them beside our framed photos of the Kaaba in Mecca.

"You are crazy if you think the President of America is going to come here!" Abdul Chacha mumbled and spat a stream of tobacco through the gap between his two remaining teeth and into the dirt. He reached into the side pocket of his kurta, drew out a bundle of papers covered in plastic, and waved it accusingly at us. We looked at each other and rolled our eyes. Not that old thing! We had seen it countless times before—it was his nineteen-year-old property deed.

The Yamuna had swallowed Abdul Chacha's land and banana trees two decades ago in one of her monsoon frenzies. That year a lot of us had lost someone or something. The government helicopters had hovered over our village for days like locusts and brought a plague of ministers. The politicians made promises of compensation in money and land, distributed deeds and compassionate smiles, then climbed into their helicopters and flew away. We didn't get a single taka or hear from them again.

Abdul Chacha was the only one who continued to write letters. But the official replies were balls of string. There was no beginning or end and finally one tripped over the whole unraveled mess. Now he didn't believe in anything. Especially good news.

"So you think that the President of America will sit under the shade of the banyan and you will all speak with him?" Abdul Chacha wagged his yellow, tobacco-streaked beard at us. "Murkho! Fools! I'll pray Allah gives you brains!" he said and stomped off in the direction of the mosque.

"They will probably make us stand in line as if we are at the ration shop. But the President Sahib will bend his head and listen quietly—as he does on TV," one of us said. He looked so sure that we too felt a sudden lightness at the thought that all kinds of bright new things would take place in Joipura in a few days.

People began arriving when there were only two days left before the President's visit. They streamed into Joipura from the nearby villages. There were young men with greased film-star hairdos; women with babies on their hips leading cows who still gave milk; and grandfathers bent over with the weight of their years. They clung to tractors, filled bullock carts, piled onto the roofs of buses that wheezed up twice a day, or swayed precariously three to a bicycle. Some walked—six, nine, sometimes twelve miles—balancing baskets of rice and dal on their heads to last them for three days.

We lined up to watch in wonder as the crowds jostled along the road, and sneezed as the red dust rose in their wake. A few of us flung a tarpaulin onto two poles and set up a table and an instant business along the dirt road. We sold pencils and cheap plastic water pistols to their children, glass bangles and bobby pins to their women, and puffed rice splashed with mustard oil to anybody who had a few taka to spare. For two taka we offered to repair the straps of their broken sandals, shave their faces, or clean their ears. Our oldest children hawked glasses of buttermilk spiced with green chillies, and then ran around with sweet sticky mishti to cool burning mouths.

We made space on our floors for our excited cousins and let strange infants sleep with ours. There were grandmothers huddled on the verandas of the post office and young men on the roof of the bank. Ishmail ordered us to allow the visitors to camp in our fields, and the smell of dried fish wafted from their fires at night. Some said there were 5,000 more people in the village. Abdul Chacha swore it was more like 10,000 fools. We didn't care. It was a mela, a carnival, and we were making more money than we had in the harvest season.

On Muhammad's TV we watched the President speak at a trade conference, press a huge red button at a new dam, and listen with his eyes closed to the wavering wailing of Baul singers. He beamed at us from the screen and we smiled back, waiting.

———

Muhammad came up with the idea of the toilet. The village officer had come to inspect the podium we had erected under the banyan tree. Ishmail, his hands knit behind his back, his head clerk with an open ledger and pen in his hand running after him like a puppy, had begun his third round around the makeshift wooden structure when Muhammad stopped him.

"What if the President wants to go . . . you know . . . for number one. Have you thought of that, Officer Sahib?"

Ishmail faltered in his stride.

"As if he'll want to go . . . He's here for some two hours. These world leader types are trained to hold it in," he blustered.

"But what if . . . He's not that young anymore. It's possible."

We agreed loudly that it was a completely possible possibility. Ishmail looked at us angrily as if it was our fault that the President might need to use a toilet.

"If he wants to go, he'll go. He can use the bathroom in my—" He stopped, struck by the same thought that had passed through our heads.

"Your office? That place is not fit for a goat," we said.

The toilet in his office was the only public one in the village. Everybody—the staff, the hawkers, every petitioner who had traveled hours to get here—used it with abandon. It stank. The smell was so bad on hot days when the wind died to nothing, it made people three rooms away gag.

"Maybe he can go in the fields with the rest of us," Muhammad said. We guffawed at the thought of the President of the United States rushing to the field followed by his security men and their guns.

"No, no. You are talking nonsense." Ishmail waved his hands as if Muhammad's suggestions were flies he could swat away.

But he looked flustered for the first time. "What can I do now? There is hardly any time left!" He almost wailed and we sniggered at the high pitch he hit.

"Umm . . ." The wrinkles on Muhammad's forehead climbed up his balding hairline. "Well, there's the toilet I started building at the school. It is almost finished. All it needs is a door really," he finally said as if he had thought of it just then.

Of course! We smacked our hands to foreheads. The money sanctioned for the school toilet had run out before the contractor could hang a door or paint the concrete walls. The children still went in the bushes around school or ran home at recess. Muhammad had stopped doing the rounds of the village office after a few months and we thought he had given up. Now here was the solution. Here was the brand new toilet we wanted for the President. For once Ishmail didn't have anything to say.

That afternoon, a few of us rode into town and came back in triumph with a shining new aluminum door. Four of us unloaded the door from the chug-chugging tractor. Struck by the afternoon sun, the metal square turned into a liquid shining thing, reflecting blinding shafts of light onto onlookers' eyes and into the downturned faces of shy girls, flashing random illumination into the trees and onto rooftops so that it was transformed from a mere door into a beacon, a broadcast, a summons that swelled the crowds around the toilet.

Many volunteers clamored to paint the gray concrete walls of the toilet. But we refused to give up that honor. We hung the door with studious disregard for the conflicting instructions shouted by wisecracking onlookers, many of whom did not even belong to Joipura. We painted the walls. The stores manager of the bank had donated leftover whitewash. There was even half a tin of brilliant blue paint for the door. Then we paid three boys a taka each to guard the toilet with their lives. When the paint dried Muhammad got a jamadar to scrub the urinal until it gleamed and placed a plastic bucket of water and a mug in the corner, even though there was a working flush. Then he locked the door with an imposing stainless steel lock and tucked the key into his pocket.

"It's like a virgin now, this toilet," Muhammad said as we stood smoking in front of the brand new toilet that evening, "a virgin awaiting her bridegroom on her wedding night." Muhammad secretly read sentimental poetry sometimes. We'd discovered that he hid the books in his office, behind the mark sheets left over from past exams. "And that door . . . painted with the blue of Allah's heaven," he continued. We turned to watch Ishmail's reaction. He looked pleased as he walked around the structure he had come to inspect. In the fading light the walls glimmered white and pristine and the sharp smell of paint came from them. The toilet was the one new thing in our village of bleached huts, tattered cow sheds, and buildings marked by generations of dirty hands.

"Let's hope the President gets to use the new toilet when he comes to visit the school," Muhammad said as we were leaving the school grounds. Ishmail stopped and looked at him. "If we want him to see it, we'll have to bring him to the school, won't we?" Muhammad said and continued walking.

We held our breath.

"Okay, okay. Half an hour—he'll be here for half an hour. Make sure that those urchins of yours wear uniforms at least tomorrow. And shove the ones without shoes to the back of the class," Ishmail said, walking away so quickly that he was almost running.

"They'll recite from their English textbook and spell 'Washington' for him," Muhammad shouted after him. But Ishmail didn't slow down or turn to see us slapping Muhammad on his back hard enough to make him cough.

That night we couldn't sleep. It seemed as if no one could. There were crowds of young men wandering around, some tying the last few banners and buntings to the trees and telephone wires, some merely hanging around smoking. It had rained earlier and the green metal chairs set in rows under the trees for the VIPs looked washed and clean. Our children were out in the streets in packs, shouting and screaming as if it was morning and not the middle of the night.

"Go home and sleep or you won't be in the parade tomorrow," we threatened, but they knew we were lying and continued playing hopscotch and football.

Kerosene lanterns hissed here and there, throwing circles of light around the carts of kabab vendors and their customers and the smoky scent of coal-roasted meat and peanuts was everywhere. The band was still up. They were giving their instruments a last polish and the glow from the lanterns dripped gold up and down the sides of trumpets, which they blew in sudden *paarrps* to entertain the crowds milling about. The village looked like a fairground. Beyond the streets, in the fields, hundreds of banked fires still glowed and we could see the silhouettes of excited, sleepless visitors scurrying about.

People stopped us to ask questions. "Is it true that the President will arrive in a motorcade?"

"Most likely in a helicopter," we answered. We weren't sure but we liked the idea of a whirling aircraft thundering out of the sky onto our village. "Be sure to duck when you see the machine. Haven't you seen how they do it in the movies?" We were holding court and it was intoxicating.

"Be sure to bring a handkerchief to wail into," Abdul Chacha shouted. "Since when does America keep its promises?" We booed loudly.

"He will step out of the doors and the security fellows in their black suits will jump out beside him, their hands on their guns," Muhammad said, ignoring the bitter old man. "There will be hundreds of police and then a fleet of Toyota Crowns will bring him and all the ministers to the end of the street where the children will be gathered and the band will play and we'll follow the President as he walks up through the village past the bank and the podium to the school."

"And maybe even the toilet, don't forget the toilet," we reminded him.

Late that night, tired of all the excitement, we walked home in a daze. One by one we stopped talking, silenced finally by the amazing thought that in just a few hours the President of the United States would be here, among our huts and paddies and duck ponds, hearing our voices and smiling at our children.

The President was scheduled to arrive at 11:00 a.m. By seven, villagers settled thickly around the podium, squatted in the school yard, blocked the entrance to the village, stood on the roof of the bank. The crowds took over any place where they thought they could catch a glimpse of the great man. The children in their green uniforms were lined up already alongside the band. Muhammad paced nervously at the head of the columns, shushing any child who dared to speak above a whisper. The red-and-blue ribbons around their wrists fluttered in the cool breeze. Even Abdul Chacha stood outside his house dressed in his best black punjabi.

Ishmail sat in his office in his pressed safari suit, waiting for the call from Dhaka that would tell him that the President was on his way. His jeep stood outside, its engine idling so that not a minute would be lost in starting it. The phone hadn't rung yet and we hoped it wouldn't go dead at the crucial time. We hung around his office, peering in through the windows often. We didn't want to miss a moment of this day.

The phone rang at 10:30 and Ishmail sprang to his feet before answering it. He listened for a long time, then spoke once or twice before gingerly placing the receiver back on the hook. Then he walked to his jeep, ignoring us standing around it. He climbed in and sat for a few minutes without touching the gears, as if he wasn't sure where to go first. Then he revved the engine and drove off in a screeching hurry to the podium. There he didn't switch the engine off or get out, but half leaned his body out of the seat and around the windshield, just far enough to make himself heard.

"The President is not coming the United States Secret Service decided the flight from Dhaka would be too dangerous that's all they told me I don't know anything else so don't blame me," he bellowed at the uncomprehending faces turning slowly at the sound of his voice.

Then he wheeled the jeep around and raced down to Muhammad and the children at the other end of the village.

There he did the same thing, shouting his terrible message, not daring to get out of the jeep, afraid perhaps of being stoned. Then he drove back home, shut himself up behind closed windows and refused to come out for two whole days.

No one stoned Ishmail's house. No one burned his jeep or ransacked his office. Once the news spread, we persuaded the bewildered crowds to trickle off the roofs and the verandas and the school buildings.

Muhammad walked through the columns of gathered children. "The President is not coming," he explained. "He cannot come here. They think there is some danger to him, he is an important man. No, I don't know what danger. Yes, it is very sad. No, you won't be able to salute the President, Ibrahim. I am sorry I don't know why. No one told me."

He had to say the words many times but finally all of them, even the tiniest sniveling four-year-olds, understood. He declared a holiday; our children straggled back through the village with dejected faces and dispersed reluctantly. We couldn't look them in the eye when they came to us later for answers.

The worst thing was the silence that came over the village. That 10,000 men, women, and children could be so quiet, that the unruly young men of yesterday could be so quiet! That was a marvel. On the radio they said that the American Secret Service had specific information that it would have been harmful for the President to travel to Joipura that day. He had even canceled his visit to the Tomb of the Matryrs. If only they had given us a chance to tell him that no one wished him ill.

As the day progressed, many of our visitors picked up their blankets and their now empty baskets of rice and dal and started walking back to the villages they had come from. Some stopped to watch us as we dismantled the podium with a crowbar and reached up to tear the buntings off the trees.

Muhammad sat far away from the activity under the banyan tree. Some of us sat with him, not talking, just there. It was as if someone had died—what was there to say now? Finally, Muhammad threw away the cigarette one of us had offered him.

"It would have been nice to show him all that we have done . . . We too are trying to join the world here," he said. He looked around at the poles stripped of their buntings, the torn paper rustling forlorn in the breeze. "He is a great man—his attention would have made a big difference."

One visitor on his way home tried to comfort him. "Well, at least I can tell my grandchildren that there was a day in my life when I walked seven kilometers and almost saw President Clinton. That alone makes it all worthwhile, doesn't it?" he said, shifting his baby to a more comfortable position on his shoulder.

"They are attacking the toilet!" someone yelled in the distance. A crowd of people rushed past us heading for the school. We sprang out of our chairs, took up our crowbars, and ran after them. As we approached the school we could see a throng of men, jostling and pushing each other.

"Let us through, let us through," we shouted, and shoved hard at the resisting bodies until the crowd parted.

"Leave my school alone," Muhammad pleaded in panic. We were prepared to find anything, some awful atrocity committed by the disappointed masses. As we burst through the crush of the crowd, we saw a long line of men stretching across the clearing of the school yard.

We stopped at the edge of the humming crowd. Urged on by Abdul Chacha a young man was smashing the lock of the toilet with an iron rod. The metal of the door showed through the gashes on the bright blue paint. Even as Muhammad yelled, "Stop it," the lock burst with a clang. The men roared and punched the air with their fists. Abdul Chacha pulled open the door and entered. He closed it carefully behind him and moments later we heard the thin gurgle of the flush. When Abdul Chacha emerged from the toilet, he smiled at the watching men before turning to pat the door thrice, as if in approval. Then he stood courteously aside. His young helper, the black-and-white scarf around his neck fluttering, was next. Before he stepped in he turned to wave to the crowd and they cheered as they stood in their line, waiting patiently for their turn.

The Curry Leaf Tree

Dilip Alva had always possessed a most sensitive nose. Since before he came to America, long before he had even imagined the country, sprawled and waiting. Back then, in the discordant days of his childhood, if people whispered and nodded together as he passed by, it was only because of his nose.

Dilip was from Mangalore, a South Indian district famous for its coconut macaroons, among other things. Not that his family had ever tasted any, being dirt poor. His father was a ticket collector, given to harassing passengers on the unimportant, bullock-cart slow, meter-gauge trains. He was famous in the villages strung along the meandering rail lines for his unpredictable temper. Like a mad dog, the villagers would mutter, you never knew whom he'd bite next.

His father's reckless explosions earned him enemies and abrupt transfer orders. His insulted bosses couldn't fire him. The railway unions were powerful and thought nothing of disrupting miles of lines to protect their own, even a cussed and contrary specimen like Alva senior. So his bosses bounced him around from one goat-infested village station to another equally blighted. All this moving around meant that there was never enough time for Dilip to settle into an education. The meager lessons he learned in one English-medium school were soon washed away in the looping gurgle of the vernacular, which was often all the one-room school in the next village had to offer. Dilip grew up alone, torn away from classes before any boyhood friendships could leaven and rise. Most of his classmates were only interested in following him around, barking and shouting "Son of Mad Dog." His mother did what she could to redeem his dismal childhood. She exploited his nose.

His mother, Sheila, was a cook, an artist, who arrived in every new village with her instrument, a blackened cast-iron cooking pot lashed atop her bags and bundles. Soon, whenever there was a wedding, funeral, or baby-naming ceremony in the neighborhood, she'd be there at four o'clock in the morning— a one-woman catering establishment, a maker of feasts—barreling her way through hillocks of diced vegetables, overseeing the weighing and mixing with narrowed eyes, shouting precise orders over the grinding of masalas.

As he waited to be summoned to exercise his unique talent, Dilip would wander around the dark, smoke-shrouded cooking shed. Scattered around him in that dim universe would be copper plates, some smaller than a woman's palm, some larger than a car wheel; perfect disks filled with red chilli powder, yellow turmeric, coriander leaves, creamy mounds of grated coconut. His nose isolated them—the tight whirls of sharp, bright coriander wrapped into the pungent flare of pepper surrounded by the expanding corona of garlic—and drew the melange of smells deep into his center until he grew full and radiant with the knowledge of his special blessedness. Only he could help his mother hold each flavor buoyant and individual, delicately poised in the exact balance the curry needed to travel beyond greatness, to become the masterwork that people woke up and yearned for in the middle of the night. At least, that was what his mother said. And Dilip believed her.

Soon his supreme moment would arrive. At his mother's command he would stand before the bubbling cauldron of cashew nut curry or okra fugath, a thin boy in loose gray shorts, his hair and bony bare chest slicking instantly with sweat from the heat. At her nod, he would point his nose (bumpy, short, a scatter of blackheads) downward and breathe deeply of the rising steam.

"Not enough cumin, Mother," he'd pronounce. "A little more pepper," he'd say. Then, and only then, would Sheila adjust ingredients until the curry tasted exactly right.

Finally, when the cooking pots had been scoured and upended against the wall like the full bellies of fat men, the host would come up, smiling and expansive, to where mother and son waited at the back of the house. His mother would push Dilip forward to take the extended bills.

"I couldn't do it without my boy, you know," she'd say. "He has a most exceptional nose, an excellent nose." The few stragglers standing around to eavesdrop would nod their pleased confirmation and the ladies of the house would ruffle Dilip's hair as he left.

When he was fifteen, his father was sent to Kabada, a village which, it seemed to a bemused Dilip, had a feast every day of the week. After six guarded months at the local Catholic school he finally allowed himself to make a friend—Manohar Shetty. The boys explored the cave-pierced hillsides around the village and wrestled each other in the thin sand at the river's edge. Alva senior stayed out of trouble and Dilip helped his mother make more money than she had made in years. Then, just as people were beginning to recognize Dilip enough to stop him in the street and make solicitous inquiries about the well-being of his nose, his father called a supervisor a sister-fucking son of a whore and the Alvas were once again banished to the remotest village the Indian Railways could find.

The morning after the transfer orders arrived, Dilip stood in front of the cooking pots, waiting for the familiar, accurate messages about spices and sauces. But his nose was cold, uncooperative, suddenly illiterate. A few hours later, lightheaded from breathing too hard, desperate, shivering with loss, Dilip finally acknowledged the awful truth. His nose had been reduced to cartilage, mucus, septum. His talent was gone. Knocked out. As irretrievable as a milk tooth.

Here one could come up with psychological interpretations of the armchair variety. Cite cases of this or that brought on by sudden emotional trauma and so forth. Perhaps it was some form of hysteria. Perhaps it was revenge. "One minute I could smell, next minute kaput—dead nose," is how Dilip tells the story. It wasn't quite so drastic, of course. One minute his nose could sense fine details, nuances, subtleties, bottom notes and top notes. Next minute he could still smell. But in general terms. Broadly. Coarsely. Like the rest of us ordinary nose-twitchers.

Dilip stormed out of the cooking shed and returned home at 1 a.m. He woke his mother, asleep beside his congealed dinner, and blurted out the terrible news. He would never ever accompany her to a cooking shed again, he swore, as if all this was somehow her fault. Poor Sheila. As expected, she cried and pleaded. Dilip wouldn't relent. His mother recovered; after all, she was used to sudden and monumental changes. She found Dilip a boarding school far away from his father. The strict Jesuit priests who ran the school helped him find solace in the certainty of mathematics and taught him to be proud of things other than his nose.

By the time Dilip got out of college, India was in thrall to computers.

Six year olds, when asked on TV what they wanted to be when they grew up, lisped "computer engineer" in dutiful mimicry of their parents' hopeful exhortations. Dilip found a safe, well-paid job with the government. He tested financial application packages that analyzed state budgets and recommended more computers be shipped to mismanaged government offices in remote towns, where they lay unused until they became obsolete. He saw his life unspooling serenely, the rewards of hard work—a Vespa scooter, a Sony TV—accruing slowly over the years of small promotions and festival bonuses. Until a recruiting agency approached him.

He did nothing to win his appointment as a computer programmer for Motorola Inc. except turn up for the interview. The recruiter sweated in his gray suit in Bangalore's heat and sounded like an announcer on *Voice of America*. He was the first white man Dilip had ever spoken with, and he never quite understood why he of all people was selected. But once he converted his American salary into rupees and watched his mother burst into joyful tears at his good fortune, he didn't care.

When he finally arrived in Scottsdale, he didn't like it. He dismissed the Indian grocery: "What kind of stupid shop doesn't carry whole mung dal?" He had to drive too far for Bollywood videos. He was lonely. There was only one solution, he decided.

He asked his mother to find him a wife. His mother (who had fasted every Wednesday since Dilip had turned twenty-one so that he might find the perfect bride) muttered over photographs of girls the marriage broker brought her in response to her matrimonial advertisement ("educated, wheatish-complexioned, reasonably well-off") in the *Deccan Herald*. She settled on Vanita Paes.

"Only daughter. Well-known family. Father ex-military. Own house," she said in her newly adopted telegraphic style when Dilip called. It was her way of trying to save Dilip money on international calls. His mother's breathless ecstasy careened off Dilip's ear and set up a tinkling happiness in the center of his stomach. A woman out of the scattered, mysterious, scented millions was about to become his wife.

Dilip rushed back to India for a full unpaid week, just twelve months after he had arrived in the States. He was prepared to fall flamboyantly in love.

The parlor windows of the venerable Paes house overlooked the kitchen garden with its tomato plants, pumpkin patch, and sole curry leaf tree. While the various fathers and uncles in the room talked the cautious, polite, probing talk of men about to become relatives, Dilip watched the woman who was about to become his wife.

Vanita came out of the kitchen and walked up to the curry leaf tree, reached up and plucked off the leaves, gently pulling at each stem where it fused with the branch. It had rained earlier and the tree shuddered droplets onto her pale blue cotton sari every time she touched it. It took her a long time to gather a good-sized bunch. Only then did she turn around and look straight at Dilip. A tall, slender girl with skin the color of milky tea and curious, unafraid eyes, holding the dark green curry leaves like an offering under her chin. In the soft, diffused light of early afternoon the scene, the girl under the tree, seemed to Dilip straight out of a romantic Hindi movie. She walked past the window with her head bowed in deference to the elders in the room and a tendril scent from the leaves floated in. Dilip sat there smiling. Then a cousin nudged him and he put his young-professional-from-America face back on. He knew then that he wasn't good enough for Vanita, that her family would never have considered him eligible without his American job and his American car. By then, however, the first sight of her and the dense, faintly citric scent of the curry leaves had undone him.

Vanita Paes could not cook. She had a degree in literature, she had visited London, she could denude her eyebrows like a professional—but she could not cook.

They were in the dal aisle at the new Spice Coast Supermarket when she told him.

Their first week in America had been blissful. They had done the usual things honeymooning couples do—sightsee, take pictures. They created indelible records of themselves, sunburned and sweaty, squinting into the sun in the Sonora Desert, in front of the Heard Museum—every single place Vanita had marked in her *Lonely Planet* guide. Dilip, incapable of resisting her pouting, had even, for the first time in all his months in Phoenix, tried Mexican food. (He hated it. Too much cheese). But in a few days he would have to go back to work. It was time, Dilip had urged, that they got down to the serious business of married life. Stocking up on Indian groceries was only the beginning.

Dilip placed the packet of yellow lentils in his hand carefully back on the shelf. "Can't cook? You must have picked up something from your mother?" he said.

"My mom? My mom doesn't *cook*." Vanita sounded affronted, as if he should have known this about her. They had been married for twenty days.

"Doesn't cook," Dilip repeated. He had never heard of such a thing. Were there mothers who did not cook?

Dilip knew Vanita had lived in army bungalows with army gardeners and army maidservants. He hadn't reckoned on army cooks. Why hadn't his mother quizzed her about this most fundamental of wifely skills?

"Three, four—that's the fourth time you've opened and closed your mouth in the last few minutes. See! I said you do that—but you wouldn't believe me." Vanita teased. Then, seeing his stricken face, she paused. "You can cook, can't you?"

Of course he could cook. He could cook in his sleep.

"Then we're fine, aren't we?" Vanita said, and shrugged.

Now here they were a week later, together in the kitchen at 6 a.m. staring at a pound of dead bird.

"So I am to learn kori curry before you leave for work." Vanita poked at a limp chicken breast with her knife and shuddered when it slid wetly off the plate on to the countertop.

"The fastest way to peel garlic is to press on it hard with the flat part of the knife. Like this," Dilip demonstrated, ignoring her petulance. "Here, you try." He smiled and handed her the knife. He had vowed to be strict but forgiving, imagining this was how gurus behaved when they were about to impart wisdom to a deserving pupil.

An hour later they were still at the second stage, onion-frying. Vanita had nicked her thumb with the knife prying the meat of a coconut from its shell. Dilip waited patiently while she poured half a bottle of Dettol on the wound and wrapped a Band-aid around it. He didn't point out that it really was a tiny, tiny cut.

"The onions," he reminded her when she came out of the bathroom.

She slashed at the onions in the saucepan with her spatula, held awkwardly in her unhurt left hand.

"Gently," Dilip said. "You have to stir them gently so that each individual slice separates and browns evenly—you can't rush it. Every bit of the onion needs its moment in the—" Dilip stopped. Vanita was glaring at him.

"You are going to be late for work," she said.

"My mother ground spices for five hundred wedding guests on a stone."

"So now you want me to go down on my knees and thank Jesus for the blender?" Vanita said.

"You are angry. I don't mind. Really. I understand learning something new is hard," he said. He did not raise his voice. He put the blender in the sink. "Now why don't you put the chicken pieces in. Stir them until I finish my bath," he said and left the kitchen.

That was Monday.

On Tuesday he taught her bengal gram and tendli curry. On Wednesday, a simple capsicum fugath. He woke her up at 6 a.m. as usual on Thursday to teach her the difference between nigella seeds and mustard seeds ("one pops, the other doesn't). Mutton with cilantro on Friday, and with the idle weekend hours unfurling ahead, a feast on Saturday—white pumpkin curry, prawn fry, coconut dosa, and pork vindeal.

In the weeks that followed, there were mornings when, waking up to his new wife warm and rosy beside him, he was tempted to linger. But he, Dilip reminded himself, was a man who had gone from being the son of a village cook to a software engineer making $85,000 a year in America. He was not easily deterred. Even when faced with someone as stubbornly opposed to learning (Dilip had to reluctantly acknowledge this fact) as his wife.

Two months passed in a blur of recipes and confrontation. Then, one Sunday, soon after he had attended a rousing Mass that left him eager to continue his work of enlightening the ignorant, Dilip Alva's superior olfactory abilities returned with all the power they had possessed in his childhood. He was bending over a wok full of pungent shrimp gassi when it happened.

One sniff and there it was. Swoosh! Like sinuses clearing up!

Dilip stood transfixed, his ladle frozen in mid-descent. He cautiously angled his nose at the gassi again to make sure. There it was again, each flavor leaping into his nose like a shard—sharp, pointed, clean.

He turned to Vanita chopping onions at the counter.

"I can smell," he whispered. He wanted to kneel. Give praise and thanks. Laugh. Weep.

"If something's burning, it's your fault this time. You're the one near the stove." Vanita looked up, tears running down her face.

"I can smell," Dilip shook his head in wonder. After all these years of fuzziness, clarity. It was a miracle. A divine reward for educating Vanita.

"Oh, good. I can too." Vanita, knife held aloft, dashed her sleeve against her eyes. "Most humans can, in case you hadn't noticed," she said.

"Every clove, every seed, every thing that is in the curry—even what is too much or too little, I can tell just by smelling." Dilip said.

"You're crazy," Vanita said, something poetic and declamatory in his tone finally catching her attention.

"Not crazy," Dilip shook his head. Alive, he thought. After all these years, alive.

Vanita ignored him. "I knew it. All this nonstop cooking. Of course! That's the answer. You are stark raving mad," she said. Her face crumpled. "My family was cheated. I am married to a madman," she wailed. She liked being dramatic. Until a few weeks ago Dilip had found it all charming—her flounces, her head-clutching.

Dilip put the ladle down (Vanita stepped back warily) and drew himself up in front of the shrimp gassi, like a man about to jump off a cliff.

"Watch," he said. He closed his eyes and stood with head lowered for an instant, as if lost in prayer. Then he bent slowly from the waist over the bubbling pot, inhaled, and straightened up just as slowly. His indrawn breath swelled his chest. "Poppy seeds. Mustard. Onions. Garlic. Curry leaves. Chilli powder—a bit more is needed. Fenugreek, for sure half a teaspoon too much," he listed, his voice firm and strong.

Then he opened his eyes and looked at Vanita. Her mouth was open. The knife hung limp at her side. He waited for her to say the words.

Her mouth flattened into a laugh. It was not a nice laugh. "Is that supposed to impress me? You *know* what goes into the shrimp. Just half an hour ago you yelled the ingredients out to me from the living room. You were relaxing on the sofa watching the basketball game while I—." She stabbed the knife in his direction for emphasis. "I ground and chopped and stirred." "Remember? And now you pretend to have some kind of gift for deconstructing curry." She rushed over to the stove and turned off the burner, as if to forestall him from repeating his performance.

He had left her alone with the gassi to build her confidence. But that was hardly the point.

"So you think I am making this up?"

Vanita didn't hesitate. "Yes," she said.

"There's something you don't know about me," Dilip said. "Something I never told you." Vanita's expression changed instantly into horror. She expected only the worst from him—murder or madness in his family.

"I was the best smeller in every village I ever lived in," he said. "People far and wide praised my nose."

There. It was out. The biggest thing that had ever happened in his life, the happiest and the most painful, laid now at her feet for safekeeping. He wondered if this was one of those turning points in a marriage that people talked about.

Vanita narrowed her eyes and thrust her face forward as if waiting for him to say something else. Then she burst out laughing. Then, noting his expression, laughed even harder. "Is that it? This is your big secret? That you smelled things?"

"Not things. Curries. My mother was a cook and—"

"Your mother was a cook!" Vanita stopped laughing. "I thought she managed a catering service."

Dilip hurried on. It wouldn't do to get sidetracked. "Did my mother tell you that? She lied. She was a cook. Anyway I smelled the curry and told my mother what it needed to be better. Then one horrible day it was gone, just like that. I thought I lost the ability forever—and now, just now the shrimp gassi brought it back." Dilip felt the joy of that earlier moment flare in his middle again.

Vanita struggled to maintain her shocked expression at his revelation about his mother and failed. She staggered, spluttering, to the dining table and collapsed into a chair.

"So your grand contribution was the sniffing?" she said and snorted. Dilip was sure. His brand-new bride, his curry-leaf girl had snorted at him.

"Business must have suffered when you had a cold!"

———

When the alarm rang at six the next morning, Dilip didn't bother to get out of bed. He ignored Vanita's raised eyebrows when she walked in to the kitchen an hour later and saw him scowling over a bowl of cereal.

"What! No culinary razzle-dazzle this morning? Don't tell me you have taught me everything in your repertoire," she said.

Dilip winced. His wife used words like "repertoire" and that, too, barely out of bed. He got up and set his half-eaten breakfast in the sink. "Cooking is not simple." He bent down to find the brush he kept under the kitchen sink and polished his shoes. Then he stood up and smoothed his shirt front. "You have to be always curious, like a spy. Have the patience to lean on the table and see what happens. Every time, something different comes out. Even if it is the same kori curry you have made twenty times, every time it will be little different from what you expect. That is the fun of it."

"You are lecturing," Vanita said. But she said it without heat. She looked faintly surprised.

Dilip grabbed his briefcase and walked toward the door. He paused with one hand on the doorknob. "I am not going to teach you anymore. From now on you . . . you do alone. You must have learned something by now. Even you can't be that bad," he said and ran down the stairs before Vanita could say a word.

Dilip masked his surprise when Vanita actually began making dinner. And she did it all alone. Not once did she phone him at work to ask, "Is that one teaspoon of coriander powder or one tablespoon? I can't read my handwriting," as he expected her to. In fact, she didn't speak to him at all. She lay the table in silence and they ate in silence. Dilip felt cheated—he should be the one sulking after the way she had behaved and the things she had said. But he was determined not to speak—even when her offerings testified to a sad fact. He had spent the better part of his newly married life introducing her to the food of his ancestors for nothing. She did not have the "blessed hand," as his mother liked to call it.

Things went on for days in this fashion until she made his favorite chicken ajadina. They were sitting down to dinner when Dilip peered under the cover of the dish.

"Too much cinnamon," he said. The words popped out, an old habit suddenly getting the better of him.

"You sniffed," Vanita said. She snatched the lid from his hands and slammed it back on the dish. "Seven nights now you have sniffed."

"What are you talking about?" Dilip picked up a serving spoon and stuck it into the rice bowl.

"I felt sorry about the other day. I thought I'd show you that I had in fact learned something—that you were not the only accomplished cook in the world. And I did, didn't I?" She reached across the table and grabbed the serving spoon from him. "Stop! You answer me. Didn't I?"

"Yes," Dilip said.

"But all you do is sniff! You sniffed at the dal and spinach, at the eggplant, at the beef fry and the—"

"We don't have to go through every meal," Dilip interrupted, unwilling to revisit painful memories.

"You even go into the kitchen the second you come home and open the pressure cooker. You hover over it, briefcase in hand." Vanita dropped her nose within a few inches of her plate, closed her eyes, and swayed her torso, breathing strenuously.

Dilip thought she looked ridiculous.

"You look ridiculous," she continued. "You think I don't see you? I'm standing right there, behind that door watching," Vanita jerked her head in the direction of the bedroom door. "Trying to find fault—that's what you are doing."

"Yesterday, the ginger-garlic paste for the beef—too much ginger. I knew the second I walked in. It was in the air. But not one word did I say, did I?" Dilip stretched his hand and tried to take the serving spoon back from her. She held it down. They wrestled for it briefly.

"You don't have to say anything, your face says it all. Well, I tell you one thing, mister nosey nose, I am not going to suffer anymore. No more cooking. I refuse." Vanita, her knuckles tight around the spoon, ladled rice onto her plate furiously. Then she served herself the chicken and started eating.

"Millions of Indian women don't touch one morsel also until their husbands have tasted the food," Dilip reminded her. She made him say these things, he thought.

"They can all starve for all I care." Vanita paused with her hand halfway to her mouth. "You are doing this just because I didn't believe your bull about your nose."

She took a bite of chicken, chewed, and swallowed. "This is good chicken notwithstanding the cinnamon." She looked at Dilip. "You are living a lie. If only you could hear yourself. I saw you performing for Mala the other night at dinner. Since then neither she nor Vinod have called. What do you expect? I am sure we are the laughingstock—"

"Mala challenged me, remember? She said, you'll never guess what's in the spinach." Dilip was trying for a reasonable tone. Vinod and Mala were his closest friends. Who better to share his good news, his returned talent with?

"She didn't actually expect you to grab the dish from her and stick your nose in it. And then the seventeen things on the table weren't enough for you. You had to make her pull out leftovers from the fridge!"

"Four. Mala made four—"

"Four, five, a hundred . . . Who cares? The worst part was, she was encouraging you—oohing and ahhing like an advertisement."

Dilip said nothing.

"Mala's husband does card tricks to impress people." Vanita picked up her plate and rose from the table. She looked close to tears. "And you? You sniff at pots and pans at our friends' homes!"

The next night at dinner, there was a square white box lying on the table.

"We are having pizza for dinner," Vanita said cheerily. There was so much he didn't know about his wife, Dilip thought. Here was a woman capable of serving mass-produced cheese-covered pizza, out of spite. What else could it be? This, after he had invited her to share the one thing he had loved the longest—the aromas of fine Manglorean food.

Over the next few days, they ate oriental chicken, seafood lasagna, chicken pot pie, mushroom risotto.

Vanita had discovered Stouffers. Dilip remembered the first time he had left India. He had pressed up against the window on the plane and watched Bombay's spiky coastline recede until the class filled with the blue of the vast separating sea. He felt the same desolation now, the same sense of the familiar falling away.

One Sunday afternoon, the microwave meals exhausted, the couple went to buy sandwiches at the Subway near their apartment. Dilip didn't want to go. He disliked American food and such places made him nervous. He hated answering the staccato questions the gum-popping teenager behind the counter flung at him. White bread or wholewheat? Turkey, chicken, or beef? What kind of cheese? Onions? Olives? Red pepper or green? The questions made him say all the wrong things, struggling to make his mind up fast enough, asking for beef when he wanted turkey, blurting out whole wheat though he hated it, huge holes opening up all the while on the surface of his careful composure.

Even as he hung back, Vanita went up to the counter.

"Hey, how's it going? I'll have a foot-long, white, turkey, cheddar, pickles, olives, hot peppers, and hold the mayo, please," she said.

When Vanita made room at the counter for him and sat down at one of the gleaming chrome tables all he could do was stammer, "Same for me."

That night, he lay on the couch feeling sorry for himself. He should have known. The signs had been there, only he hadn't seen them. In the months leading up to his wedding he had called Vanita every week. He had asked her all the usual unimaginative questions. Her friends, her schooling, her interests. But all she had wanted to talk about was America and he had struggled to explain this glittering, lonely country that he did not understand.

After Vanita had arrived, Dilip had stopped caring that he wasn't invited to the weekend barbecues and trips to the casinos in Vegas that he heard his American colleagues discussing on Monday mornings in the cafeteria. He had convinced himself that together he and Vanita would make sense of this country. But here she was serving Stouffer's and conquering Subway—obviously, she had made more sense of it than he had.

Mackerels brought Dilip back. Fresh mackerels from the Oriental Market—red-gilled and lustrous, smelling not of fish but of the sea. Rubbed twice with salt and rinsed under water, they flashed silver from the kitchen countertop. Dilip could not stop himself. He assembled the ingredients: coconut scraped moist and milky from the shell; whole seeds of coriander and dried red chilli, lightly toasted on the griddle; tamarind pulp; fresh ginger and serrano chillies, sliced slim. Onwards then. The chopping flowing into the roasting, and then, the blender roaring dully in the background, the mustard seeds stuttering in hot oil, Dilip turned choreographer. His hands flying between counter and stove top, his fingers reaching blindly but unerringly for a scoop of cumin, a pinch of turmeric, knowing without thinking how to mute the harsh jangle of the coriander with the blandness of coconut, how to lay surprises for the mouth to stumble upon: ginger, tamarind, and the sudden heat of the serrano.

Then in the midst of this concatenation, a singing, certain feeling. This was what he loved best, this wondrous world of scent and steam that had so recently been returned to him. He would not give it up, not even if it meant losing the first battle of his fledgling marriage. It wasn't even that he wanted a traditional wife, someone who would stay home and attend to his every need. He had hated it when he was growing up—the freshly ironed shirt laid out on the bed, the slippers ready by the door, his mother struggling to stay ahead of her husband's demands. He wanted small things. Onions and grated coconut browning slowly in oil. Tamarind soaking into peppery pork. Fermented sanas plumply steaming. The aromas greeting him like a warm hand on his chest when he walked in the door after a hard day. In the endless, arid months before his wedding, Dilip had dreamed up the perfect marriage. His vision did not include teaching his wife to boil water.

But if Vanita didn't want to cook, he would. And if his wife thought him less of a man for it, then so be it.

His decision made, Dilip immediately felt better than he had in days. When Vanita came home from her Tae Bo class, Dilip had already laid the table for dinner. The fish had pride of place. He had found some papads in a corner of the fridge and fried them.

He was getting ice out of the trays when Vanita started deep breathing over the fish.

"Not enough salt," she said and picked up the salt shaker. Before Dilip could say anything, she unscrewed the bottom and dumped the entire contents onto the dish.

A few days later, Dilip and Vanita accompanied friends to the Republic Day celebration organized by the India in America Society. Saris in the colors of the flag—green, orange, white— fluttered from the ceiling. There was a faint whiff of potato samosas waiting in the wings.

Mrs. Mathur, the wife of the wealthiest Indian in Phoenix, stood in the middle of the banquet hall, a crowd around her. The men wore silk kurtas, the women gold-trimmed saris. Vanita wore jeans, the only woman in the room not wearing Indian dress, Dilip realized, and was instantly irritated. Who had ever heard of a bride not wearing a sari? She did it to annoy him. One more thing. They had hardly said three words to each other since the salt incident.

As Dilip and Vanita tried to squeeze through, smiling politely, Mrs. Mathur reached through a gap in the crowd and grabbed Dilip's arm.

She must have been at least sixty, but to Dilip she looked

nothing like any old lady he knew back home: tall, polished cheekbones, short gray hair, a pearl necklace down to her navel.

"Dilip Alva, isn't it? And this must be Vanita," she hollered. Her voice was the only fat thing about her. "I'd like you to come to dinner this Saturday."

Dilip opened, and at a nudge from Vanita, closed his mouth. He felt anxious. Why him?

Within days of his arrival in Phoenix, Dilip had learned that there were only two castes of Indians in the city: the ones who owned homes and the ones who didn't. Homeowners clustered together at parties bemoaning property taxes and swapping names of reliable gardeners. The rest clung together at the other end and aspired. Like Dilip, they were almost all computer types, still uneasy about the country, resolutely working their way up from the Honda Accord and the DVD player. And although the homeowners deigned to mingle with them at these patriotic celebrations, the property-deprived knew that there were more intimate gatherings—poolside barbecues, catered brunches, and meet-the-famous-singer parties—that they were excluded from.

"So what do you say? Around seven okay?" Mrs. Mathur boomed, thrusting her face close.

The crowd was waiting for his answer, their envy pulsing silently against his ears. What else could he say?

"Yes. Okay. Of course," he managed.

"Awesome," she said, like a teenager and smiled. All of a sudden she looked impish, more eccentric aunt and less scheming soap-opera heiress.

Then, just as Dilip turned to leave, she bent down even closer. "And don't forget to bring that nose of yours."

"Mala." Vanita whispered, when Mrs. Mathur had sailed past, taking the crowd with her. "I am going to kill her."

On the drive home, Vanita bit off and chewed a freshly manicured nail tip. She broke her silence as they were getting out of the car. "See! I told you," she sighed. "Laughingstock."

Mrs. Mathur revealed all the moment their small party was seated at one end of the immense dining table. It had elephants carved out of teak for legs, Dilip noticed, and immediately felt the back of his neck prickle with sweat. He stood up to tell Mrs. Mathur that he had a blinding headache and had to go home.

"Mala said you were stupendous, a sight to behold," Mrs. Mathur drawled. Dilip sat down. "I just had to see for myself. It sounded like terrific fun."

And what Mrs. Mathur wants, she orders, Dilip thought, quelling the reflex to glance at Vanita. He wouldn't give her the chance to shake her head no at him. If you want to be an entertainer join the circus, she'd said, imagining debacles even before they had turned into the woman's driveway. I swear I will leave you if you do, she had said. Fortunately, just as a nervous gurgle began in his middle, two Hispanic maids dressed in identical pink saris walked in with bowls and platters of food.

The aromas escaping from the numerous covered bowls climbed up his nostrils and lightened his head. They washed warmth into the cold hollows of his stomach. Dilip first felt calm, then a sudden clarity. He could stop this now if he wanted to, disappoint Mrs. Mathur, quietly eat his free dinner and go home. But this strange old lady, their odd host was right. Ahead lay adventure. And yes, for one final time he would be the digger and delver, interpreter and unraveler, the one to shake out the whole cloth of the dish and point out each shimmering skein. He stood up, scraping his chair back against the floor. Vanita looked up at him stricken, a woman being propelled toward certain social annihilation. There are ten thousand Indians in Phoenix, imagine all of them smirking about us, she'd said yesterday. He walked slowly around the table. He began with a covered platter set close to Vanita. Aubergines. Charred over a naked flame and minced, their smoky meat spiked with green chillies and cilantro, gentled with yogurt.

Dilip played his part. He closed his eyes, he breathed. He felt himself grow sure, confident. "Eggplant. Smoked. Perfect," he said, eyes still shut tight. "Bravo," Mrs. Mathur said.

Dilip stopped wondering what he was doing at a table where prime ministers had dined. The leg of lamb rubbed with cumin and lemon spoke to him, and he translated aloud. He forgot that half an hour ago he had been intimidated by the procession of cutlery beside his plate. He cracked the basmati rice with Goan sausages in two breaths, right down to the paste of cloves and cardamom that perfumed the rice. He refused to look at the contents of dishes, only raised the lids a sliver. He sipped at the scents, swirled them in his nostrils, exhaled noisily. He detected nuances, subtle accents, mere whispers of flavor. Someone, perhaps one of the maids, stifled a giggle. Dilip didn't falter.

He worked even faster, almost sprinting around the table on his short legs, the hair on his forehead flopping, panting out the ingredients before it left him, this lucid confidence, this billowing state of grace.

Mint. Poppy seeds. Bitter melon.

Lifting lid after lid.

Lemon rasam. Steamed shark.

Bobbing and swaying. In breath. Out breath.

Breadfruit. Roasted chickpeas. Asafoetida.

Mrs. Mathur swiveled her head to follow him around the table, her face excited and happy, like a fan watching her favorite player win a match.

Dilip was nearing the end. There was only one bowl still left to uncover. He paused. Then took out his handkerchief and wiped his forehead, and folded it carefully before tucking it back into his pocket. He was trying to slow himself down, put off the end when there would be nothing left, when he would have to raise his head, look at Vanita's face.

He approached the last dish. He stopped, hesitating. He opened his mouth and then closed it without saying anything. Ash gourd and roses. Who would combine the two? Perhaps his nose, finally confused by the cacophony of odors, was sending him the wrong signals. He heard a sound from Vanita. She leaned far over the table, her face rigid with tension, her fist clenched in front of her heart. "Come on, come on," she mouthed silently. Then it came to him. He had heard of this— Gul-e-Firdaus, the Flower of Paradise. It had been invented in the palace kitchens of the Nizam of Hyderabad. "Kheer!" he burst out. It was pudding, the ash gourd rendered viscous and sweet with milk and sugar, scattered with crushed roses. Once upon a time the creamy desert would have been left uncovered on a terrace at dawn to let the rose petals on its surface catch the morning dew, an essential ingredient.

Dilip stepped back from the table. He knew it was a virtuoso performance, his best ever. But now the moment was over. Already, it was receding like the sea, and all that remained on the stripped sand was the carcasses of crabs, bottle caps, ordinary debris. The room was quiet, Mrs. Mathur still silent at her end of the table. An air-conditioner thrummed somewhere deep inside the house. He looked down at the table, the beautiful china, the hibiscus in the centerpiece, and the crisp napkins beside the plates. He heard a rustle of silk, the quiet whistle of long-held breath from Vanita. He wondered if she would get up from her chair and walk to his side. Hold his hand. He wanted her to understand that there were some things that he could not change, that he was stuck being who he was. All he could do was stand here in front of her, with his peculiarities and his passions, and hope she would recognize him wholly and completely. He looked up. Vanita's gaze swept past him to include Mrs. Mathur and the maids in her dazzling smile. Then she looked into his eyes. "Shall we eat?" she said, shaking out her napkin.

My Grandfather Dreams
of Fences

For a time when I was fifteen I was my grandfather's right-hand man. It was the place he assigned me, often literally, since he couldn't hear very well with his left ear. The day my boarding school closed for the summer I headed home to the farm. When the bus turned the corner and I saw him, leaning bareheaded on his stick, his gray hair blazing white in the late evening sun, the familiar excitement began building in me.

"Come on. I have been waiting for two hours. Your grandmother killed a chicken in your honor," my grandfather said and grabbed my suitcase from my hand and hurried off down the dirt road that led to the farm.

He never asked me about school even though I had been away for nine months now. It was as if, now that I was home, every other part of my life had ceased to exist.

"The boy is here. Take this suitcase into the house and tell his grandmother," my grandfather yelled out to the workers weeding the field near the house. One of them clambered up from the field and hefted the suitcase onto his head.

"We'll go to the pond first," my grandfather said, walking away. I tried telling him that Grandmother would be waiting but he pretended he hadn't heard me, even though I made sure I was on his right side. He hurried me to the stretches of coconut trees that lined the huge pond that lay in the center of our property.

"These are the new hybrid dwarf variety. They mature faster—the agricultural station claims they'll yield coconuts in just seven years. At least you'll be here to see them even if I am dead," he said, pointing at the green fronds that stuck up from the earth. He had refused to try them when the agri-officer had first offered them to him last summer. Bah! All these new trees are unnatural, he'd said. I wondered why he had changed his mind.

I said it looked as if someone had buried an entire coconut tree in the ground, then left the tops out because they didn't fit, and he laughed. I remember feeling relief that nothing had changed in the time I had been at school. The pond was a dark smudge amid the bright green fields. Swarms of quacking ducks shattered the purple reflections of the coconut trees in the water as they swam in frenzied circles. A short distance away I could see the tiled roof of our house rising above the mango orchard that surrounded it.

"Don't dawdle, Satish. Your grandmother is waiting," Grandfather said as we turned toward the house, as if the thought had just struck him. Some workers walked by and inclined their heads respectfully at us.

"Kochu Thamburan, you're back," they said, calling me little landlord. It was only after I had grown as tall as my grandfather that they started calling me by that title. It made me uncomfortable to hear it.

"Nowadays, these people look you full in the face and talk," my grandfather grumbled. "Some of the young ones don't even bother to take their cigarettes out of their mouths." I said nothing, wishing he wouldn't talk so loud.

My Grandfather Dreams of Fences

Grandfather stumbled on a clod of mud as we turned into the gate leading to the compound of the house and grabbed my shoulder for balance. I held my breath but he didn't take his arm away. I felt proud as we walked toward my grandmother, who stood in the courtyard watching us with a faint smile until I ran up to hug her.

My grandparents were all the parents I had. My father and mother had died in an accident when I was three and all I had left of them were a few photographs. In one they are standing on a balcony and my mother is laughing with her hands raised as if to swat playfully at my father. Her hair, loosened from her plait by the wind, blows in wisps about her face. I would sit for hours with that photograph, studying their expressions, wondering what it was that he had said to her to make her laugh like that. Late at night, I would invent their conversation to each other, the things they were saying at that exact moment, being first my father and then my mother, sometimes whispering sentences aloud alone with all the other boys around me sleeping and grunting in the dark. But that was at school. At home in the summer I slept with the loud drone of my grandmother's prayers—she claimed God didn't mind that she kept Him up late. He understood that she only had time for Him after her cows and hens were penned in for the night.

Two days after I came home to the farm it was my fifteenth birthday. In the morning, freshly bathed, the sacred sandalwood paste still wet on my forehead, I bent down to touch Grandfather's feet and seek his blessings.

"What took you so long? The fence has been moved," he barked. He did not place his hand on my head in blessing or gather me in a bear hug. He did not hand me the ten rupees that I usually got as a birthday present. "Get the tape measure and follow me. I am going to teach that son of a dog Kori a lesson," he said and heaved himself out of the armchair he had been reading the paper in.

"Fence? What fence?" I stammered, straightening up in a hurry. There were fences all over the property. They marked the boundary between the fields and the highway, between our farm and the neighbors, between where the rice paddies ended and the groundnut crop began. My grandfather found new places to divide with fences every monsoon.

In his hurry to leave the house he grabbed his cane and strode out of the door with his feet shoved into a pair of my sandals. I wasn't about to tell him they were two sizes too small. Not now. "The fence in the mango orchard—that Kori thinks I am blind. He moved the fence in the night, at least one foot. What's wrong with these damn sandals?"

Halfway down the path toward the orchard he turned and looked at me hesitating on the doorstep.

"What are you waiting for? Get the tape. And hitch those trousers up . . . They are falling off your backside." His white eyebrows bristled together like hairy caterpillars.

I hurried to the tool closet, hefted the thick roll of tape in its ancient leather case, hoisted up my brand-new birthday pants, and ran after him.

The hens scratching along the fence scattered in clucking alarm at our approach. The fence wound around one side of the mango orchard, separating our land from our farmhand Kori's backyard. His hut was set a few feet away from the fence. Smoke from his wife's cooking seeped out of the thatched roof. The front of the house, hidden from us at this angle, lay just outside the wrought-iron gate to our house and faced the dirt road that ended at the gate. The family was like a pack of guard dogs, unceasingly alert to whoever entered and left the farm. They questioned strangers and carried news of their coming to us in the big house.

In the sun-dappled shadows under the mango trees, the fence looked perfectly ordinary, just thorny twigs of bamboo lashed together with rope and hung on wooden slats. It had been worn smooth by the rains and the yellow of the bamboo had paled to mottled cream. Gray mold had grown here and there along its length, bedraggling it further. Last summer Kori and three other workers had spent a week in the bamboo stands behind our house, stripped to the waist, slashing the spiny bramble off the plants. I had stood with my grandfather under his giant umbrella and watched the exciting flash of their machetes in the sun. The men had lashed the thorny twigs to the wooden slats with rope and hung miles of new fence everywhere, including the mango orchard.

"*Da!* Kori! Where are you? Stop hiding in your wife's kitchen. I know what you are up to sneaking around at night! Did you think I wouldn't notice?" Grandfather yelled into Kori's backyard, blundering up and down the length of the fence, slashing at its twisted twigs with his cane.

I waited. There was nothing else I could do. Through the leaves of the mango trees the sky was a clear, glassy blue. In the fields beyond the orchard there were slow contemplative cows to startle. If I had left early, I could have caught a few cat-fish before everyone else crowded the river. A faint smell of dry-ing cow pats rose from Kori's backyard. His wife used them for fuel.

"Kori! Come out here right now." My grandfather's shouting made my heart race.

Kori came running out of his hut at full pelt and stumbled to a stop on the other side of the fence. After a quick look at my grandfather's red face he bent his head and gazed respect-fully at the ground, folding his arms around his thin, naked torso. Three of his children ventured out behind him dressed in nothing but ragged shorts. Kori instructed them with a slight nod to follow his example. Ramu, the eldest, who always dug up earthworms to bait my hook when we went fishing in the river, looked up at me and grinned under his cowlick before he ducked his head.

"Do you have any shame? How can you do this, you ungrateful wretch?" My grandfather was a tall man and he easily leaned over the fence into Kori's backyard. "Look," he said, pointing to the ground, "I can see where you pulled up the stakes. The ground is like butter, any kid can do it."

Last May Kori and the other men had struggled to dig the holes and pack hard mud around the stakes. He had pulled out the stakes and used the fresh soil to plug the holes. Its blackness contrasted with the clean, swept surface of the rest of the yard. The earth away from the holes was trodden down, worn smooth and gray by the family's bare feet and by the rains, which had been heavy this year.

"You!" my grandfather shouted at me and I jumped. "Measure how many inches he's moved it." I looked at him not quite understanding what he wanted me to do.

"Use the tape measure, idiot," he snapped. My face smarting, I knelt down. My hands trembled as I pulled at the loop at the beginning of the tape and the stiff metal strip straightened out. I didn't look up but I felt Ramu and the other kids watching me with interest. I pulled out a length as long as my arm, locked it into place and gingerly pushed it under the fence. It seemed somehow wrong to do this, to stick my tape under the fence and measure Ramu's yard. On the other side, Ramu knelt down and pulled the tape obligingly toward the edge of the freshly filled holes. He could read and do numbers, having dropped out of school only two years ago.

"Eight and three-quarter inches." He read out clearly. In the silence I could hear my stiff pants rustle as I shifted on my haunches. A cow lowed mournfully in the distance.

Some eight years ago when I had decided to learn cycling it was Kori who'd held the handlebars steady and jogged beside me until I learned to stay on.

"That's eight and three-quarter inches of our land that you are trying to take over." My grandfather was so incensed now that he was swinging his cane wildly about. I crab-walked quickly out of the way, pulling the tape measure after me. Ramu's youngest brother giggled. I giggled too and quickly coughed to cover it up.

"My father made a big mistake, being good to you people. Now I have a snake pit in my backyard," my grandfather said. "Pull those stakes up and put them back where they were before. And do it before nightfall." He hit the fence with his cane for emphasis. Purple trumpet flowers from the vine Kori's wife had planted along the fence crumpled down.

Then Grandfather looked down at me crouching with the tape measure in the dirt. "Come on, Satish. Are you going to sit here all day?" He marched off into the house. Following him, I looked back and saw Kori and his children filing quietly back into their hut. Later Grandfather said he was going to check on all the other fences and left. He didn't ask me to go with him.

I wandered into the kitchen and sat down to watch my grandmother churn the yogurt for butter. The loose flesh of her arms jiggled as she pulled at the chain that spun the beater.

"Don't mind your grandfather. He likes to hear himself shouting," she said, turning around to look at me. Her hair was white and reached down to her knees when she untied it to oil it. "Kori will move the fence back and your grandfather will have forgotten everything tomorrow. And I am sure he'll remember your gift later this evening." She always referred to her husband as "your grandfather."

"But why was he so upset anyway?" I wondered.

She didn't answer. In the silence the thick *shlurrp shlurrp* of the yogurt was oddly soothing. "Your great-grandfather owned whole villages," she said after some time. I had never met this illustrious ancestor, although there was a portrait of him proudly astride an elephant in one of the hallways upstairs. "He owned miles of coconut groves and mango orchards, planted whole hills with tea and forests with cardamom. He had so much land that a few square yards lost here and there didn't matter to him. Everyone talked of his generosity." She had her storytelling voice on, the familiar sing-song that had lulled me to sleep throughout my childhood. "He gave away small plots of land to various farmhands, including Kori's father. He was his foreman, you know, and your great-grandfather was very fond of him. The plot on which Kori's house now stands was given to *his* father on the day Kori was born. That's why people around here always call him Lucky Kori, haven't you heard them?"

The family had lived there, in one corner of the mango orchard, for as long as she could remember. They were there even when she came to the house as a bride. And the children had played in our courtyard and climbed our trees and fished our ponds for as long as I could remember.

"Of course your great-grandfather was the unlucky one— one fine morning the Communist government took away everything," she continued.

I heard the rusty squeak of the gate being opened and went to the veranda to look. My grandfather refused to oil it, saying it warned him of intruders. It was only Kori's wife, and she walked quickly across the courtyard with downcast eyes. She was going to our well. The family drew their drinking water from our well and she came and went many times a day, her muscles straining under the weight of the pot tucked into the crook of her arm, her clothes permanently soaked even in the cold season. It was rumored that Kori beat her. We heard them fighting often, Kori's voice incoherent in his drunkenness, rising louder than the screams of the frightened toddlers. Yet he never raised his voice or even his eyes to my grandfather—not even when he shouted at Kori as he had done today.

"Paru didn't come today to sweep the courtyard. And Kalappan says we might have to find someone else to milk the cows. Says he might get a job that gives him a bicycle." My grandmother had moved on to something else. "It's getting impossible nowadays. We'll have to sell everything and move to the city. Of course your grandfather won't hear of it, says he wants to be cremated where his mother was, under the mango trees . . ." She sighed. After a few moments she got up and stood bent over for a few minutes before carefully straightening her back.

I fetched her a bowl for the butter that was rising slowly like a new island in the whirlpool of yogurt. Her talk of selling the farm made my stomach clench even though I had heard all this before. My uncle Raman, on a visit from Bombay, had explained it to me a few years ago. It had something to do with the economy and workers' making better wages in other places. A lot of factories had opened up in our area and the workers preferred to roll tobacco into beedies or dip matches in sulfur than work on our land. It was getting hard to hold on to what we had left.

Later that day I had heard them shouting about it upstairs. Uncle Raman had some property nearby and he had sold it abruptly one day, without offering it to my grandfather first. He had called my grandfather "a blind old man" to his face, and my grandmother had cried and not spoken to him when he left, not even to say goodbye, angry with him for calling her husband names. Since then my uncle seldom visited the farm.

"Well, at least Kori is always around at everyone's beck and call," I said as I left the kitchen. This came out sounding spiteful. My grandmother didn't answer but it was true. They called him to climb up to the water tower and clean the slimy floor of the water tanks, or to clear out the attic after every harvest. When a hen fell into the well last summer, it was he who had climbed in with a basket tied to a pole and persuaded the stupid terrified bird to come out.

I felt restless and vaguely angry, unable to settle down to anything. I wanted to be out there in the fields in the sunshine but was afraid of meeting my grandfather and having him frown at me. I decided to do my summer homework—the boarding school made sure I had reams of it to finish before I went back. That would show him. Here I was, not enjoying myself one bit on my birthday, huddled over my books inside the house. I was determined to sit in the study until he came home for lunch.

The study on the ground floor had large windows that looked out over the garden and its hibiscus trees. Gray squirrels ran up and down the tree trunks, stopping for a moment at mid-branch, their raised tails quivering like bushy antennae before dashing off again. I took out my geometry set and began drawing circles. Ramu appeared at the window, standing on the broad ledge that ran underneath. My grandmother was drying pieces of coconut on it. When the white flesh shriveled, Kori took the copra to the mills to be pressed for oil. Ramu was chewing on a piece. I looked at him and looked down again.

"There's a kingfisher's nest near the pond. It has three blue eggs," he said. I drew a few more circles. He was wearing a shirt I had outgrown two years ago. Most of my old clothes went to his family. First he'd wear them and then over the years they'd appear on each successive younger brother until they fell apart.

"May I draw one?" he asked, his eyes following my hands. I

got up, pushed the book close to the window, and showed him how to hold the steel point of the compass fixed on the paper. His arm was black and wiry against the white pad. Ramu and his family weren't allowed inside the house. It didn't occur to me to question these rules, things were just the way they were. He'd always been fascinated with every new thing I brought home from the town. Now he laughed, delighted with his first attempt. I exchanged the pencil for another one from my box of colored pencils and he drew a red circle intersecting the gray one I had drawn earlier.

"So what about those eggs?" he asked me, not looking up from the paper and his busy hands. Ramu was two years younger than I but he always managed to know more. He knew how long we had to sit unmoving by the pond to be rewarded by the sight of water snakes rising and rippling across its still, green surface. In the mango season he would create a slingshot with a piece of inner tubing and a forked stick powerful enough to reach the highest mangoes. When we went down to the river to fish, he'd lead me to the exact rock under which the older, fatter fish slumbered.

"Would you like to go to a movie today?" I asked, surprising myself. I had never been to a movie here in the village. My grandparents didn't go to the cinema, deriding it as entertainment for the lower classes, and I wasn't allowed to go alone. Even as I asked Ramu the question, I was convinced that this was exactly what I wanted to do. It was my birthday. Today I was old enough.

Grandfather left with Kori after lunch to go to the neighboring town to buy fertilizer. I asked my grandmother after I was sure he would be halfway there on the bus.

"A movie?" she said doubtfully. "What'll people say, the thamburan's grandson in a movie house? They say those places are filthy."

"How would you know, you've never been. Why don't you come with—" I stopped, reluctant to tell her I was going with Ramu.

"Get out of here . . . Me watching that rubbish!" she laughed, and I knew it was all right. Later as I was about to leave, she handed me ten rupees.

On the way to the cinema, Ramu walked some distance behind me. He never forgot himself, not even once. A few laborers saw me and stood aside until I passed, making a little bowing motion with their heads. Perhaps I should have just nodded gravely as my grandfather did, I agonized after I had smiled awkwardly at them.

In the theater, which was nothing more than a large hut, I gave Ramu money to buy tickets and we sat on the best seats— wooden benches. He was pleased. Until now he'd always sat on the dirt floor in front of the screen. I bought two newspaper twists of roasted peanuts and we ate them quickly, even before the interval.

The film was full of action, the twin heroes filling the screen with high twirling kicks and sword fights on rooftops, and we walked home in the dark in high excitement. As we started to cut across the path through the fields leading to our houses, we saw Ramu's father weaving slack-legged in front of us. As we neared him, we could hear him cursing under his breath. He stank of cheap liquor. He looked around and nodded in my direction.

"Where were you?" he asked Ramu.

"At the cinema. What a film! Top class. Full of dishum-dishum," Ramu shouted. The beam from the torch in his hand swung wildly about the fields as he punched the air, mimicking the heroes.

Kori turned around and grabbed Ramu by the arm and

gave him an open-handed slap to his jaw. The torch dropped from Ramu's hand as he half fell to his knees. He whimpered in surprise when Kori cuffed him on his head again and again.

"Kori!" I shouted in shock. He ignored me.

Kori bent down and picked up the torch, turned it around, and began beating Ramu about his shoulders and arms. I could hear the metal handle thudding thickly against his flesh. The torchlight bobbed over my body, the rice paddies, the path, Kori's laboring chest.

"Who do you think you are? Who do you think you are? Just who do you think you are?" he demanded.

In the middle of the noise and the chaos, I remembered. "Stop it Kori. Stop it right now. I asked him to come. I said stop it." My voice trembled as I commanded him.

Abruptly Kori stopped. He handed me the torch without once looking at Ramu lying curled on the ground with his arms wrapped around his head. "Go home, kid. Here, take your torch and go home." He waved me away.

I tried to stand my ground, to hold his gaze and wait until he left Ramu alone. But I could not. Something fierce in his face wouldn't let me.

"Go now. Your grandmother is waiting," he repeated, scarcely audible.

I turned and ran, frantic and stumbling across the suddenly hostile fields. At home I didn't tell anyone about Kori. When I told my grandfather I had been to a movie, he merely grunted, "Good, good," and asked me to accompany him to the mango orchard. There he shone his torch along the fence to check if Kori had put it back where it belonged. He had.

That night I lay awake for a long time staring at the fireflies sparking outside my window, hating the tightness in my chest.

Ten days later the fence moved once again. I didn't need to measure it to know that this time Kori had taken much more than eight and three-quarters inches of our land. The next day my grandfather did something he had never done in all of the seventy-five years of his life. He stepped into a laborer's house. He went over to Kori's front yard and stooped to enter the low door of his hut. I stood at a distance and waited, my stomach churning with worry. I didn't know whom I was afraid for, Kori or my grandfather. I didn't hear any other voices other than my grandfather's cajoling tones in the clear morning air. I imagined Kori standing silent, head downcast, with his family grouped nervously around him. When my grandfather came out of Kori's house he went straight to his bedroom and lay down. It was the first time I had ever seen him rest in the day-time.

The next day he handed me an iron padlock and key and told me to lock the gate. The lock was old and ornamented with flowers and leaves and the key was hard to turn.

"Kori and his family are not to enter this courtyard ever again," he said when I came back.

I heard my grandmother gasp. "But you can't deny them drinking water. Where will they go?" she protested.

"I can deny them anything I want. My father only gave him that land, not our well. Let him learn. There are other places you can get water here," he said and left the room. There was to be no further discussion.

I hung around outside in the courtyard, dreading yet waiting for the moment Kori's wife would come for water. Finally, Ramu came with one of his little brothers. He stopped at the sight of the locked gate and looked at me. I shook my head and shrugged. At that moment I wanted him to understand that there was nothing I could do. I wanted him to understand that more than anything else I had ever wanted in the whole world.

In the days that followed the locking of the gate, the work of the farm went on. It was time to cull coconuts and my grandfather called in a laborer I had never seen before. He clenched his machete between his teeth and shimmied easily up the smooth tree trunk with only a short loop of rope stretched taut between his big toes for traction. I had studied the technique closely—the placing of the toes on the sides of the tree, the clutch of knees and arms—but never understood how they got up so high so quickly. My grandfather had refused to let me learn this thrilling skill. "Have you ever seen any thamburan up a tree?" he'd jeered when I asked him.

We stayed well out of the way until all the coconuts had thumped down. My grandfather and I then stuffed the felled coconuts one by one in gunny sacks. I had never seen my grandfather do things like this before. It was hard unfamiliar work and my arms ached with cradling coconut after coconut. There were only the three of us and no other laborers to carry the filled sacks across the fields into the house. The stranger asked for more money to carry the bulging sacks back.

"Do you expect me to pay you twice? Once for the trees and once for the carrying? I'll do it myself." My grandfather was beginning to lose his temper. The hot sun wasn't helping.

"Grandfather, the bags are heavy. There's no way we can do this," I said softly.

"Who asked you? I have done this before and I'll do it again. I can do without these people," he muttered.

The laborer hefted a bag onto Grandfather's head and stood aside as he walked unsteadily down the road, his legs trembling a little under the weight of ten coconuts. As we passed through the gate Kori stood watching in his front yard. He didn't go back into his house when he saw us approaching nor did he come forward and offer to help. To me that too was a new thing.

Grandfather had to lie down when we got home. I went back and paid the man to carry the rest of the coconuts home. As we made our way through the fields, I walked far behind him so I wouldn't have to see his satisfied smile.

I went down to the river by myself one afternoon. It had shrunk with the heat and gurgled placidly past the rushes that fringed it. The earthworms I had dug out wriggled about in the mud-filled coconut shell next to me. I went to the rock Ramu had shown me and cast my line. He had said that the fish underneath it were granddaddies, wily and massive with age. The sun was high and except for a few women washing their clothes further downstream, I was alone. Buffaloes wallowed in the shallows nearby, insects rising from their black shining hides like mist. I sat there for hours and the line only bobbed once: when I drew it up my bait was gone. Yet a heron mincing about on its thin delicate legs dipped its head and came up regularly with a squirming fish in its beak. Ramu and I would make tallies of the fish we saw the birds eat. I threw a pebble at the heron and it rose shakily into the air and flew off. The moment it was gone, the river seemed deserted. The heat and haze of the afternoon made me drowsy. Yet I was reluctant to go home, to the locked gate and the silent courtyard. The weeks ahead stretched emptily. For the first time in my life I wanted the summer to be over.

When I got home my grandfather stood surrounded by people in our courtyard. Most of them were young and had the trademark beards, khadi kurtas, and cloth bags of the comrades from the local Communist party offices. I recognized some of them and smiled.

"Ah! Here's the kochu thamburan!" one of them called, a false heartiness in his voice.

I walked past my grandfather and made to go into the house, but he put his hand heavily on my shoulder. I stood there feeling awkward in front of all these people, the fishing rod dangling slackly from my hand.

"Thamburan, you can't deny them water. His wife has to walk a mile now to the nearest public pump." A burly bearded older man spoke. He was smiling a lot and trying to look humble and concerned. I had seen him before. Last year he had stood in our courtyard and talked about some scheme to provide day care to the workers' children. Grandfather had gone to his big safe and given him money and Grandmother had sent me out with tea and snacks in crockery reserved for important guests.

"All Kori has to do is move the fence back," my grandfather said, sounding tired, as if he had said this many times already.

The man didn't answer. Instead he took out a piece of paper from a file and read something in it, taking his time. "He has been a laborer attached to this farm for many years. You cannot stop him from working here. I heard you are bringing people from outside to do his jobs. That really will not do." His voice was quiet and serious even if he was still smiling.

I could see my grandfather's face beginning to flush. "I can do whatever—" His voice rose, then finished softly, as if he remembered something. "—these are still my fields and my land."

"Those days are going, Thamburan, or haven't you heard?" Someone hidden in the crowd yelled and a few people laughed.

"All he has to do is return my land."

"What land?" The big, burly man raised his voice. "A

measly two feet? When you have so much what does another two feet matter. You can't even cremate a man on two feet of land," he said, his voice thick with contempt. I could see the faces in the crowd turn stony in agreement.

I looked around for Kori. He was standing apart from the crowd as if not sure whether he should be there at all.

"Let it go, Thamburan," someone else said in a high whining voice. "Forgive him. Let him keep it—what does it matter. You people have enjoyed yourself for too long." I wondered if everyone hated us.

Grandfather's hand tightened on my shoulder. "Let it go you say. That's what happened. We—we let it all go," he exploded, and I saw Kori wince. "Everything we had we had to give away, bit by bit. Now he wants to take the rest. All of them want to take the rest. But if I leave here, then we'll see who will give the lot of them any work." He was shouting now and a few people stepped back. But some others just stood there smiling scornfully, enjoying the spectacle of this stubborn old man spluttering and stammering.

Grandfather paused and when he spoke again his tone had changed, grown sadder. "My father lay there . . ." He pointed to a veranda upstairs that had a view of the fields. ". . . and watched the government surveyors measure every inch, every furrow in the fields, and note it in their books. The Communist government gave most of it away to . . . to people like him." He gestured in Kori's direction. "Sixty acres—that's all that was left for him in the end. My father never got up from that bed after that."

He stopped and I wanted to scream at him not to plead with these people. I felt him move and his hand was suddenly unsteady on my shoulder. The leader looked at me. "Go get a chair for your grandfather," he said, and the others moved aside from the doorway. I fetched a chair from inside and Grand-father sat down abruptly, without protest.

Dusk had fallen and the individual faces in the crowd were harder to distinguish. The leader sat down on a ledge near my grandfather's chair and stroked his beard for some time, as if pondering what to say next. He leaned in and began speaking in a quiet voice to my grandfather as if only the two of them were left in the courtyard. "Things are changing," he said. "Kori and the others know more than they did. They know about government policies and subsidies for the poor, and what they don't know, we tell them. There is work and there is money now everywhere." He paused. "There's only so much you can do alone." He sounded as if he was sorry.

Then he stopped speaking and they sat like that for some time, my grandfather and the leader among the gathering shadows. I heard the faint clack-clack of the well's metal pulley as my grandmother drew water in the kitchen. The white shirts of the crowd glimmered dully as a few people started drifting away. The meeting was over.

I don't remember how I spent the rest of the summer. But school reopened and I went back to the city and wrote oc-casional, bland letters home that were never answered. That wasn't unusual and it didn't worry me too much. The next summer my uncle in Bombay invited me over and I spent three months awestruck by the city. My grandparents weren't happy but decided it would be good for me.

When I came back to the farm two summers later there were new fences all over the farm. They had sold the cows and the chickens but somehow my grandfather had found enough people to build fences for him. There was one that began with the intention of protecting a gooseberry tree, but only com-pleted a semicircle around its trunk; then it meandered along the edge of the pond, climbed over a small hillock and around a few haystacks, and abruptly ended right in the middle of an old pasture, as if my grandfather had suddenly remembered an urgent errand. There were unfinished fences everywhere, the bamboo faded and mossy, the ropes frayed, the stakes listing in the wind. Most of the bamboo was gone, cut down to build fences that went nowhere, guarded nothing. As I walked around bemused, I saw workers hurry past with their heads down, not looking at me or acknowledging me. Kori hadn't been invited back and my grandfather had to go as far as the next town to get people to work on the farm. Some rumors implied Kori was dissuading the locals from coming to the farm because he wanted to force my grandfather to take him back.

My grandfather gave vague orders from his armchair and didn't stand in the fields under his umbrella anymore. He took naps in the daytime, sometimes going to bed straight after breakfast. I was sure everyone did exactly as they pleased and robbed him blind.

As for Kori, he had a concrete house in place of his hut. My grandmother said he had applied for a loan the government gave to help the poorest people and he got 30,000 rupees. His house had two rooms and a tin roof. Kori and his children had built it themselves and now Ramu was finding work as a mason's assistant, she reported. She was thinner and complained more often of pain in her knees.

On my second day there I went into the mango orchard. The cloying smell of spoiled fruit was everywhere and clouds of engorged flies buzzed here and there in an ecstasy of feeding. My grandfather hadn't found anyone to harvest the mangoes this year and all that was left was waste and rot. I turned to leave, my gorge rising with the devastation of it all, and then I saw Kori's fence. Only it wasn't a fence anymore but a high brick wall cutting across the orchard. There were no purple flowers climbing up its sides. The surface was unpainted and gray and already stained with lichen in places. The two feet of land that Kori had taken, the one thing that he hadn't been given by anyone, still lay inside it. Kori had finally found a piece of the earth to call his very own.

That evening I persuaded my grandfather to take a walk around the fields with me. The coconut trees stood black against the deep orange sky of late summer. A few farmhands, the day's work done, were walking home, hurrying their squabbling children along. We both saw Ramu coming toward us on a bicycle. My grandfather stiffened and looked away immediately. Ramu slowed down when he saw me and his bicycle wobbled and I thought for one glad moment that he would stop but he didn't. He was a few feet past us when I called out his name. I didn't stop to think and I heard my grandfather make a strangled sound next to me. By then Ramu had jumped off and stood waiting until I walked up to him.

"I hear you are a good mason now," I said, not knowing what else to say. Years seemed to lie between us, not just a few months. He smiled. I walked ahead of Grandfather, and Ramu wheeled his bicycle alongside me. It was new, with red plastic covers on the ends of its handlebars.

"The ledges along the sides of the house have cracks and need resurfacing," I said, and waited for his answer. He hesitated, then glanced at me sideways.

"Is Thursday all right? There's something else I've contracted to do until then," he said.

When we reached his house, he lingered outside politely until I walked on. Dusk had quietened the fields and emptied the pathways. I stopped beside our gate to wait for Grandfather. In the falling light the land around us was fading, its outlines thinned and insubstantial as it merged with the night.

A Certain Sense of Place

Suni was afraid of arguments. She always left the room when people began raising their voices or shrank into a corner and smiled brightly at everyone as if that would make the noise go away. So when Jai heard Anita arguing loudly with the manager as he entered the hotel lobby he was surprised to see Suni standing beside her. Jai dropped the bags he was carrying and hurried over to the reception counter.

"We booked these rooms a month ago and you can't turn around now and say we have to share a room." Anita thumped the desk for emphasis and Suni flinched. Jai was momentarily amused at the picture they made—Anita inches taller than the manager peering up at her, Suni cowering yet resolute, holding onto her end of the counter with whitened knuckles. She now smiled with relief to see Jai.

"You was to report at twelve thirty a.m.—it is written on receipt. It is busiest season and you are very, very late," the manager said, putting aside the fat pen he had been using to scroll down the ledger. He turned to Jai, ignoring Anita. "Nothing I can do. You'll have to share room, sir," he shrugged.

"This bureaucratic little runt is nuts. It's not our fault that the goddamn bus broke down twice is it?" Anita argued. Jai put a gentling hand on her shoulder. The bus ride up from Madurai had been long and she was tired. Plus it bothered her when things fell out of the order she had put them in in her head.

It was almost dusk. Jai could see the dimmed gray surface of the lake below him through the bay windows that ringed the room. He was glad that soon it would be too dark to see anything—in the morning the view would be a surprise. He hoped Anita wouldn't make too much of a fuss. He wanted very much to stay here.

"There's nothing we can do right at this moment," Jai said under his breath. Next to Anita, Suni stopped biting her nails to open and close her mouth nervously.

"Suni, ask someone to move our bags, will you?" Jai said wanting to put her out of her misery. She gave him a grateful smile and hurried off.

The manager's eyes darted between Anita and him and Suni and looked away. Jai knew he was speculating on the nature of their relationship.

"Could you put an extra mattress on the floor?" Jai said quickly. Maybe the guy would find them another room in the morning.

"Mattress no problem, sir. But room, big problem. Fully booked for the weekend." The manager turned to unhook a set of keys from the board behind him.

Jai glanced down at Anita. She was glaring at him.

"It's too late to find another place," he said, and picked up the keys the manager had put on the countertop. "You'll make Suni feel awkward," he added softly. After a moment Anita moved away from the counter.

Jai nodded politely to the manager. "Goodnight. Pip pip and tally ho, girls," he said heartily and walked over to Suni and the bags.

Suni giggled. The three of them had played at being British the entire afternoon, all the way up the mountain, answering each other with loud "Jolly goods" and "Blimeys" and struggling to keep straight faces. The middle-aged lady in the seat across the aisle had leaned over twice to stare at them. Suni had come up with "Gob smack me with a kipper!" and insisted it wasn't her fault if they had never heard such an expression. Somehow, visiting Kodaikanal, it had seemed natural to evoke the British.

"I am sorry about this, you guys," Suni said when they were in the room. She was rummaging in her open backpack and didn't look up. "Having to share . . . maybe we can find another hotel in the morning."

Suni was anxious about intruding. Tonight she'd probably lie awake worrying, her insecurities in full bloom, Jai thought, watching her bent head.

Anita glanced at him before she turned to Suni. There was a faint red crease on her cheek where she'd put her head down in Suni's lap to avoid being bus-sick over the endless hairpin bends.

"Stop it, Suni. This is not your fault. Jai and I can go without for three nights." Anita grinned at her, making an effort to reassure her. "Goose!" She swatted at Suni playfully and Suni smiled back, but her eyes returned to Jai's.

"It's quite all right, old girl," he boomed at Suni in his best BBC imitation. Suni smiled and turned back to her unpacking.

The rest of the evening Anita was quiet and withdrawn, still unsettled and sulky over their arrangements. Jai decided it was best to let her sleep it off and stepped outside the room onto the wooden porch that skirted their front door. A few minutes later Suni followed him outside.

"She's just tired," she said after some time, almost to herself.

Jai nodded. Suni always felt the need to defend and explain

Anita, even to him. Jai sometimes wondered if Suni ever tried to make excuses for him to Anita.

"I am okay, Suni. Get some sleep . . ." He smiled at Suni and soon she squeezed his arm and went back into the room and closed the door.

Jai leaned against the railing. The air smelled of the hills. The scent of eucalyptus oil and leaf smoke had been everywhere, from the moment the highway had first curved into the mountains toward Kodaikanal. He'd always liked the way the word sounded, the hard "Kodai" sliding into the fluid "kanal."

Kodai had been a colonial town, born out of nostalgia and make-believe. High above the sun-struck plains of South India, the British had created Kodai in the image of the quiet green pastoral towns of England. Here, among the soft rolling hills and tame woods, they built their homes with wraparound verandas and neat hedges and set them far back from streets named after memories—Glendale, Charing Cross, Primrose Lane. Now the graceful lines of the old buildings had been compromised by pink hotels that thrust their brash facades up between ivy-covered stone walls.

Their hotel was a holdout. Once the official residence of the governor, it had kept its garden and the massive white columns of its portico intact. Jai wondered if they still had the cucumber sandwiches and scones they'd served at the high tea of his childhood.

Precisely two days before he went back to his boarding school in Bangalore, his mother would wrap herself in her prized blue pashmina shawl and ask the driver to drop them off at the hotel's entrance. The bowed old waiter in his gold-trimmed uniform would recognize them and hurry over the moment they walked in.

"Raisin scones with jam, cucumber sandwiches, and Darjeeling tea, please. The same for the boy," his mother would order without looking at the menu.

On Jai's fifteenth birthday his mother had invited his father to come along and for once he had agreed. That was the last time the three of them had gone to high tea together. His father had ordered the pastry tray to be brought to their table and asked Jai to choose. Jai had hesitated for minutes, his fingers hovering over the three-tiered silver stand. In the end he had picked a pale yellow lemon tart. He hadn't thought of it in years, of the three of them together in one place, the wind coming off the lake making a mess of his father's hair.

His father had died a year later when Jai was on vacation in Nepal. A few months later his mother had decided that Kodai's winters were too cold for her. She hadn't asked Jai before she sold the house his father had built and moved to Bangalore. Jai felt the old resentment churn in his stomach. He had avoided coming back for twelve years. All of a sudden he was glad Suni and Anita were here with him now.

The governor's bungalow had been renamed Garden-on-the-Lake, probably the invention of some ad-agency creative like himself. Jai grimaced in the dark. Advertising was so much bullshit.

An owl hooted softly high in the trees. Jai took a deep breath of the cold, scented air and turned to go back inside the room. The windows of the room overlooked the lake and he had drawn the curtains back earlier. Anita was sitting up on the far side of the king-sized bed with the moisturizer bottle on her lap, sliding her fingers up and down her slick, creamed arm in quick strokes. She looked withdrawn, absorbed in the sensation of her fingers on her skin, intently watching her own hands. Then she put the bottle away and tied her long hair away from her face in one quick motion, her breasts rising under her silk shift.

She picked up her book and lay down. She read even after they made love, claiming she could only fall asleep if she read, even if it was only half a sentence. Once he had flung her book across the room but it hadn't changed anything. It's me, not you or us, she'd said, by way of explanation.

On the side nearest the window, Suni lay on the bed, her eyes open and staring out straight at him on the porch. Jai jumped. How long had she lain there watching? Then he realized that she couldn't see him outside in the dark. Only he could see them, the two women in bed in the gently lit room, not caring to draw the curtains, safe in the knowledge that he was out there on their tiny wooden porch. He wanted to be in the room with them in the muted light. He watched until Suni's eyes drooped; when he finally went inside, they were both asleep. He had never slept in the same room with Suni before. He switched off the lamp and lay awake in the silence listening, trying to distinguish between the quiet breathing of the two women before he too fell asleep.

Next morning, the garden helped Jai persuade Anita to give up the idea of moving. Just the sight of the lawn that tumbled in terraces from the edge of their porch to the rim of the lake, its fall punctuated here and there by old, large-leafed trees, was enough for her. She and Suni spent an hour examining the terra-cotta monkeys and rabbits that lined the steps that led down to the lake, ferns sprouting like green hair out of their hunched forms.

Later Jai sat outside on the lawn and waited for the girls to finish changing. The garden was empty except for a blonde reading in the sun. Anita was the first one out.

"The guide should be here any minute," Anita said, coming over to sit beside Jai on the grass. She smelled of shampoo, something citrus. Jai realized the blonde was watching them over the edge of her book. People did that when they saw them together. Anita often commented wryly that the two of them resembled the models in the ads they created—tall and sleek and expensive-looking. Jai slipped his hand under Anita's shirt and stroked her back in slow circles. Her skin was cool and faintly goose-bumped.

Anita rested her head on his knees and stared at the lake as if mesmerized by its glitter. The vast bowl of pale blue water, incandescent with sequins of early morning light, stretched to the foot of the far mountains. A lone cream-and-orange shikara boat glided by, a couple lying side by side under its fringed canopy. Jai's arm tightened around Anita's shoulders. This place was enough to drive one crazy. We should go back to the room, throw Suni out, lock the door, and stay there the rest of the day, Jai thought.

"I'll get Suni." Anita jumped up and dusted the back of her shorts. "She's such a slow coach."

Anita probably had their day neatly sliced up, Jai thought, watching her run up the steps. On their way here, she had written down the towns they were to pass through along their route. Every time the bus stopped, she looked down at the name on her open pad, reassuring herself.

"Don't sit there too long, Jai. We need to get going," she now yelled from the top of the steps. She was in a good mood, which was a relief.

In the beginning, they'd been teammates working twelve-hour days at the ad agency. They had kissed, almost as a joke, after a frenetic all-nighter and suddenly everything had changed. Jai had pursued her and for a while she had resisted, afraid that an affair would destroy their friendship. Even now, after fifteen months together, she wondered aloud what would happen when *it* was over. Her convictions about his eventual betrayal irritated him. He told himself he should be deeply hurt.

He got up from the grass and started up the steps. Anita thought of herself as inviolable and he did nothing to threaten her idea of herself. He didn't push for anything she didn't want to give him, didn't dig deep. So she felt safe with him. He had enjoyed the hide-and-go-seek in the beginning. It had been exciting.

Suni ran down the steps from their room and almost bumped into him. "Jai, the guide is here and he's gorgeous." She put a hand on his chest to steady herself, laughing a little at her clumsiness. There was a faint sheen of sweat on her upper lip.

"Where were you?"

"Wandering. There's a cherry tree right behind the hotel. Have you seen it? I wish I remembered something of my childhood, some detail."

Suni had been born here, in a house she couldn't wait to show them. Her parents had left, moved to Bombay when she was three. After Jai got to know her better he had pictured her as a little girl in her mother's arms or playing outside on some quiet side street while his seven-year-old self ran past with a crowd of yelling friends. His imagined scene changed often. Sometimes Suni fell down and cried and he picked her up. At other times she swung on a gate aimlessly waving, just for the pleasure of moving her hand.

"Come on, Jai. Anita'll get mad at us for being late," Suni grabbed his arm and hurried him to where Anita and Victor waited in the hotel's portico. They were going to walk the forests.

Victor the guide, as he introduced himself, was a small, pale brown man. The matted ropes of hair hanging down to his waist were tied back neatly with a thick rubber band.

"A mountain Rasta," Anita whispered to Jai behind Victor's back.

"He's too old for you," Jai told Suni as they set off. Victor was ahead of them, showing off his hill-climbing stride. They were on the trail that led to the shola, the evergreen forests that ringed the town.

"He also said that he washes his hair only once every three months, otherwise he gets headaches," Anita said, grinning at Suni's moue of disgust. "Think of that when you lust after him."

Jai was sure Suni had never dated anyone regularly. At least not since she'd met them. She would have told Anita if she had. And Anita would have told him.

Suni stopped and stood on the path beside him, catching her breath from the climb, gulping air with her long neck stretched out like a gawky bird. Suni—short for Sunayana, Sanskrit for "fine-eyed one." He wondered if her parents had ever called her Sunayana.

Suni's mother had suffered from bipolar disorder. She had spent her childhood dreading the moment when her otherwise normal mother switched to someone who disconnected the phone, stopped cooking and bathing, and lay alone in a darkened room. Suni's dad had sent them back to her grandparents and sent money to appease his conscience. Jai only knew the bare bones of the story. Anita was always the one who knew more.

Ahead of Jai, Victor displayed the forest proudly.

"See yellow-breasted wagtail, see thrush, madams," he pointed to the birds like a salesman.

He stopped near a bush with stiff upright leaves topped with conelike yellow flowers.

"There is king's candle, not real candle, plant only," Victor said, laughing at his own joke. Suni turned around to catch Jai's eye.

Everything about Suni seemed awry and slightly off-key. Her limbs were always trying to escape her, her arms stuck out at odd angles when she walked, and her long legs never quite tucked in properly under her. At parties, she could be depended upon to knock over someone's beer. Yet she had those amazing eyes. Cow eyes. Anita and Jai had called Suni that within days of meeting her. Suni, a new recruit, had been late for an important creative team meeting. Jai—harried as usual, running late for the next meeting—had snapped at her in front of all the others and gone on to the next item on the agenda.

Afterward, she'd waylaid him in the corridor outside the conference room as he hurried past. She stood there holding out her thumbnail sketches to him, her hands shaking. I have to have your go-ahead on these, she'd said, and didn't budge until he'd looked over her work.

Her sketches were startlingly good and he had been curious about her. He'd apologized for being an asshole and invited her for a drink with him and Anita after work. In the pub, Anita and she had talked about growing up without siblings; about the big city helping them find their place in the world; about the graphic concepts in Ray's *Aparajito*. Suni had shown them where the director had repeated domelike shapes in each famous scene of the film, drawing blotchy frames with Jai's fountain pen on a napkin.

A few months after they met, Anita and Suni got an apartment together. Suni adopted Jai and Anita without reservation. Jai realized that it was something about them being a couple that reassured Suni. Jai and Anita. Anita and Jai. She coalesced them into a unit, indivisible, interchangeable. They were her designated hand holders and picker-uppers, her instant family.

In her mind, the three of them balanced perfectly in some flawless equilateral triangle of friendship. Suni had invented her own place in their relationship and guarded it fiercely. In her head, Jai was her best buddy. He was good for playing pool with, for dragging to dog shows, for arguing over campaigns. But Anita—Anita was what stood between her and the world.

Anita had discovered that the only thing Suni was confident about was her art. Suni lived in the world convinced that it needed to be navigated with extreme caution because bad things were just waiting to happen. Anita had made Suni her pet project. Jai had gone along. Suni was easy to have around; it wasn't hard to make room for her. To Jai having her to witness their relationship somehow made it more real.

They were climbing higher and it was cold, but only when they stepped into patches of shade. Anita came up beside him and he reached for her hand. Eucalyptus gave way to mimosa and tall wattle, orange fungus mottling their trunks like rust. Some trees had fallen over in the monsoons but continued resolutely to grow. Dark green cushions of moss yielded under Jai's fingers and he felt grateful to be there, under the sunlight-silvered trees. It was like being in a cathedral—one felt the need to be respectful, silent. He wished he had remembered to bring his scribbling pad along. Lately he had started writing again, tentative sentences that he hoped would knit into a paragraph, a chapter, a story. When he went back and reread them they felt real, more tangible than all the slogans he coined so easily.

Anita pulled her hand out of his to pick up a bright red leaf.

"I am hungry," Suni said, walking up to them. Jai side-stepped so she could walk in between them. He found it amusing how Suni always managed to stay between them. She liked to talk to both of them at once, and he liked catching Anita's eyes over her head.

Anita and he had created Suni between them. After being alone together, they'd been fascinated by her. They'd pieced her together—taken the parts she'd told Anita and matched them up with the pieces she had shown Jai.

"Shall we stop and eat, Anita?" Suni asked again.

Anita nodded absently. Jai looked at her and knew that she was drawing it all in, the leaves and the slanted light, and the sap oozing out of the pink rents in the bark of the trees. Drawing it in and putting it away inside her to be looked at again some other time. Perhaps she would tell him about this day, her mouth hot against his ear some night, suddenly out of nowhere giving him that small part of her to hold. One tiny piece of her that he could call his own.

The next morning Anita didn't want to go to look at Suni's old house.

"You can't do that. Suni'll be hurt," Jai argued.

"I just want to sit here in the sun and read my book. I'll go again with her. Suni said it's close by." Anita's body had compacted itself into the hollow of the rattan chair. The apparatus of her day—water bottle, sunglasses, novel—marked a boundary around her. She had this ability to quickly claim a space for herself, make it her own. She would enter a room and seek a corner and pull it around her, staking out its edges with a wide-spread skirt or cast-off shoes. Her legs were drawn up under her and the wide soft neck of her cream blouse exposed her collarbones. A finger laid along the hollow would touch cool, smooth skin.

The last time they'd made love Jai had been ferocious.

Greedy. Wanting to consume her, break her down. Anita hadn't said a word then. She brought it up a few days later, right in the middle of slicing eggplants for dinner in his tiny kitchen. He had frightened her, she said. "Don't ever do that again." He hadn't said anything and she'd turned back to the stove. She thought she could contain whatever it was that had broken loose with that one sentence. Now, she and Jai could go back to the place they'd been before. Over the years of living alone and carving out a career, she had learned to dole herself out in cautious teaspoonfuls. Here is this look, this touch, this feeling that I had this morning—this should last you a week. Little bits were what she had to give. Anita was a meteorologist of the self, watching herself for sudden changes with a stern exactitude.

"Don't do that," Anita said, shifting in her white chair, squinting up at his face. "I hate it when you do that, just stand there staring at me, thinking thoughts." She put on her sunglasses. "Why don't you guys go and see the house now? Then you can be back in time for lunch."

Class dismissed, Jai muttered to himself, walking away.

"I have directions on how to get there," Suni said, taking a piece of paper out of her pocket. Her mother had come to Kodaikanal as a bride and lived here with her engineer husband, she said, as they walked down the drive.

Suni's old house when they got to it had faded dun-colored walls, streaked with mildew. It was tucked a retiring distance away from the lane it was on. A red clay driveway led up to a veranda that ran alongside a round lawn ringed with pink and purple flowers. There was an iron lock on the gate, although the battered tricycle on the veranda suggested the eventual return of an owner. Dry leaves filled a stone birdbath in the middle of the lawn.

Suni hung over the gate and watched the house, not saying

a word. The lane was quiet in the sunshine and Jai could hear insects buzzing in the bushes. Far away a car hummed faintly along some hidden highway.

"See that tree?" Suni pointed to a rain tree that towered near the back of the house. Vines clambered up from its roots, holding the trunk prisoner within their pale webbing. Suni leaned over the top of the gate, angling her body into the strange space of the courtyard, trying to see farther. "My mom's bedroom must have been back there," she said, pointing to the green-shuttered windows. "She told me that when she lay on her bed she could see a few branches dipping down at the very edge of the window. But she would think of the rest of the tree, waiting outside. She said it comforted her."

The gate had grown a thin skin of green moss which left streaks on her palms. Suni didn't notice. She sat down on a hummock of grass next to the gate and Jai sat down with her, the two of them leaning against the warm stone wall.

"My father had to go down to Madurai often. She was alone a lot . . . and it was a big house. I was born here, you know. In that bedroom with the tree." She smiled, her mouth stretching to meet the tears that seeped out of her eyes. Suni didn't turn her face away from him to wipe her cheeks and he slipped his arm around her shoulders.

"When did your mom tell you all this?" he asked.

"Many years ago. Before she got so sick. She'd repeat the story often."

This then was her story, Jai realized, this legend of her beginnings that her mother had given her. This had somehow shaped her, her mother's version of this nondescript house and the ordinary life that had been lived here by her parents. She must return to it in her mind, to this place and the house and her birth, which completed the family.

"We had a picture. In an album. Me and her, standing by the

gate with the house behind us in black and white. She's smiling, just a little . . ." Suni put her arm around his neck, resting against him. He wanted to put his other arm around her and pull her closer, but he sat still, afraid of splintering the moment.

"Did she like Bombay?" He didn't want this slow, intimate unfurling to stop.

"She was afraid of the city . . . She would lock and bolt the door the moment she let me in. Got my father to fix six locks on the door." Jai could feel her shaking her head against him. Perhaps all that time she had felt contempt for her mother. Or pity. "I had to lock all the six locks when I came home from school. Somehow doing that every day . . . locking and unlocking, it made her fears so real to me." Suni was crying in earnest now, as if the old hurt and bewilderment were made real again. "I'm sorry, Jai," she sighed, her voice thin and moist in her throat. "I don't know why I'm—"

"Shh . . . It's okay." He pulled her to her feet and turned her into his arms.

He held her, his cheek against her hair. She felt slight, the bones of her shoulders curving into his chest. He cupped her chin and raised her face up, searching her damp reddened eyes and streaked cheeks. She was bared and revealed, more exposed than she had ever been. The corner of her mouth was wet with tears and tasted of salt when he kissed it. Her mouth moved under his for a long instant. He brushed her hair away and kissed her neck, kissed her cheek below her earring.

"Jai," she said softly. "Jai." She stepped back out of his arms. He looked at her. She smiled wanly, looked away. Then she brought her eyes back to his. "We should go." She cleared her throat. "It's almost lunchtime—I told Anita we'd be back by lunch."

Jai felt panic as Suni stepped off the curb and into the lane.

She was leaving. Following her down the road back to the hotel he felt off balance, uprooted, unable to focus on putting one foot in front of the other. He tried to form a sentence, talk about the bicyclist who had just passed them ringing his bell loudly, but it was hard to find the words or get his voice to work. Suni stopped at a roadside tap to wash her face, then dried it on her sleeve. She walked faster. Jai wanted to tell Suni to stop, to tell her to sit down right there on the grass curb they were hurrying past. He didn't want to talk just yet, he decided. They would just sit quietly for a few minutes.

"Could we—" He stopped. What? Start over? Begin? Suni stopped and looked at him and shook her head no. She was pale and her mouth trembled. Then she came up to him and took his arm firmly. Her palms were damp.

"Come on, Jai. Anita'll be waiting. Victor said he'd pick us up after lunch." She walked beside him in silence, her steadfast hand on his arm, until they found Anita, impatient and hungry in the restaurant.

"Are you okay?" Anita asked Jai. He nodded quickly as Suni asked her for their map. Anita didn't bring it up again, though Jai caught her glancing at him worriedly once or twice.

Victor picked them up in his jeep. He stopped at the foot of a hill, miles away from town. Today he would serve them absolutely five-star views, he said.

Eight thousand feet above the town, they pushed through the brush to an overhang that jutted out over the evergreen forests that lay far below them in the gorge.

"Only bear, bison, deer there," Victor said, gesturing toward the valley floor covered in green and russet trees. "No man has went there. Ever."

"That's a good thing," Anita said. She looked happy.

Clouds lay in frozen tumult below them, bunched up against

the edge of the hill. One broke away and rose up to drift moistly through them. Anita hooked her arm around a rhododendron bursting with dusty red flowers at the very edge of the cliff and leaned her body over the empty air of the valley below. The wind blew her blouse into wings against her side. Jai imagined her insubstantial and transparent, launching herself gently off the cliff to float away with calm eyes and quiet smile, her shorts exposing the scar in the crook of her knee to the sun. Suni and he would watch, he thought, as she darkened the tops of the trees, just another shadow among the other shadows cast by the clouds.

"Anita! You'll fall!" Suni yelled shrilly, shocking Jai. "Stop it. Jai! Ask her to stop it."

Jai held out his hand and Anita took it and stepped away from the edge.

"Your hands are trembling," Anita said. "I'm sorry, you two." Then, lingering until Suni and Victor had gone on ahead, she said, "Kiss me" to Jai, as if she had affirmed something at this particular edge of the world.

That evening Anita made reservations for dinner at a little restaurant they had discovered, run by an escapee from civilization and the Delhi Hilton. There was apple crumble and guest books full of jottings from grateful Western travelers relieved to find familiar tastes in the bewildering mish-mash of India. Anita decided to take a shortcut Victor had shown her, an unpaved path that fell steeply from the side of the road.

"The trick is to walk diagonally across the path, first to the right and then to the left." Anita did her instructor voice and set off downward, not waiting for Suni and Jai. She'd joined a mountaineering club for a while, going off alone with a backpack on weekends until she'd tired of all the endless practice with crampons and ropes. "Never walk straight down, never run," she called up. Gravel skittered as she began to zigzag downhill.

"Maybe we should have stayed on the road," Jai said. It was getting dark.

The blossoms on the peach trees at the bottom of the slope seemed to cling to the edge of the evening sky. A few drifted off the branches, faded white, the ghosts of flowers. Anita got to the bottom quickly. Jai was almost at the foot of the hill when Suni wailed from somewhere above him, "I'm going to fall."

He looked back. She stood immobile halfway down the path, her body stiff and angled like a slanted exclamation point. To Jai, the path leading up to her looked frighteningly steep from below. "Jai, Anita, I can't do this—I'm going back up." Suni sounded terrified.

"Suni! Goose! Didn't I just show you how to walk down?" Anita yelled up at her, laughing a little. "What's with her? Is she fooling around?" she asked Jai.

Jai stayed where he was, transfixed, suddenly angry. Was Suni pretending?

"I can't move . . . I can't . . ." Suni stretched out her arms as if to grasp at air and hold it, hold anything to her. She looked as if she would topple over.

"Anita, we have to get back up there." Jai started climbing back toward Suni.

"Walk up the side, near the grassy edge. It'll be easier," Anita said, her voice trembling slightly.

On his climb back up Jai slipped a couple of times but clutched the grass and kept his balance. "Suni, sit down and lean back on your hands," he shouted as he got closer.

"I can't . . . I'll fall." He couldn't see her face clearly in the gathering dusk.

"Suni, look at me," Anita shouted up from below. There was no trace of her earlier fear in her voice and Jai felt better. Suni moved her head slowly in her direction. "Okay, just look at me, don't look down at the bottom. Now, sit down slowly." Anita sounded firm and calm.

Suni lowered herself to her haunches. Jai recalled the movies he had seen where they talked people off skyscraper ledges. But this was just a stupid shortcut, not a setting for high drama. For God's sake, he muttered.

He was close to her now. If she moved to the side, she could hold onto the scrub and grass growing along the edge and they could get her to walk back up to the main road with them.

"Suni," he said. She looked at him and looked away, back toward Anita.

"We'll all just sit here until you feel better, okay?" he said. If anything happened to hurt Suni he would die. "Suni, I—"

"Suni, sort of drag your left leg to this side. Then drag your butt after it." Anita, who had come up rapidly behind him, now leaned over into the path, one hand held out, the other anchored to his shoulder.

Suni did what she was told.

"Good. Now your right leg," Anita continued. "God, you are such a goose."

Anita was smiling now and Suni smiled back, a tiny smile. She knew she was safe now. Watching the two women, Anita talking softly to Suni, Jai felt suddenly bereft.

"Don't hurry, you are doing fine. Just keep sliding toward us," Jai told Suni. He needed her to look at him, to acknowledge his presence.

Suni was close to the side of the path now and Anita put out her hand and pulled her onto the grass. "There. That's it. Got you." She hugged Suni. Suni looked shaken, ill.

Anita's fear quickly turned into anger. "You are the biggest idiot there is. Why do you behave like that? Such a baby. Goddamn scaredy-cat."

They got off the shortcut and walked slowly down the road to the restaurant, keeping Suni between them, Anita still scolding her. Jai opened his mouth to tell Anita to shut up. His eyes met Suni's and he closed it. Suni was smiling faintly, as if she was happy just to be there, being put firmly back in her place.

That night, Jai watched the moon climb up and tack itself to the top of the tree outside their window before he got up and walked to Anita's edge of the bed and lifted the covers. She was awake, as he had known. Then there was only the urgent turning, molding, and fitting, only the quick rasp of hands and a place to rest a mouth against. There was a knee wedged smoothly around his hip and breath poured into his collarbone. As he moved into her, there was another shoulder he could see dimly, Suni's sleeping silhouette against the glass and the gray lake beyond. With Anita quickening against him, that was all he had left—the dense curve of her nearby, the shadow of her substance, filling his vision until the silent, gasping end.

Vishnukumar's
Valentine's Day

He hated the restaurant from the moment he saw the waiter. Wore an earring like a bloody woman. A tiny dagger made of metal, pointing down at the guy's shoulder. "Ray," his nametag said. Sent Ray back to the kitchen right away to get them all water with ice. Not that he was thirsty or anything, just wanted a minute to settle down without the guy breathing down their necks. Slow down, Vishnukumar, easy now. Don't spoil the Big Night. Especially since Shanti had suggested this restaurant as a change from the place they had been going to for the last fifteen anniversaries.

"Insolent Waiter Drops Water on Famous Patron," he said to Shanti, watching the guy swing his way back to their table, a tray of glasses held aloft at a jaunty angle. She didn't smile as she usually did when he did his headline thing.

"But you're not famous," Anand piped up. The first words from the boy the entire evening and this is what he says.

"Millions of people read your father's editorials every morning," Shanti said.

Good woman! He was allotted only the third edit, mostly about inconsequential things, musings on the nuisance of buffaloes on Tank Bund road and such, and the circulation was only 50,000 or thereabouts—but she'd never really grasped the little details. Which wasn't such a bad thing really, come to think of it.

"Madonna's famous," Anand said, unwilling to let the point go. The boy was getting positively garrulous, two sentences already and the night was still young.

Vishukumar agreed he wasn't as famous as the pop star just yet. Not a flicker from Shanti. What the hell was the matter with her anyway? He'd agreed to come here, hadn't he, when they could have been at good old Moti Mahal where the naans were greasy but he could lick his fingers and no one would care. Here they probably had a sign around somewhere: No Finger Licking Allowed. Ha.

All right! Time to stop pretending not to look at the artful nudes on the walls and concentrate on the menu. The food was tarted out in ornate explanations.

"Cauliflower alishaan," he read aloud in his best All India Radio voice to Shanti. "Lightly sautéed cauliflower in an aromatic tomato broth, subtly enhanced with a mélange of spices— what crap! I'm sure it's the same old rubbish—ow!" Shanti gave his foot a shove under the table to shut him up.

The waiter was standing over them, his pencil hovering over his pad, like a wasp coming in to land. Shanti stumbled so much over her order, it was painful. It wasn't absolutely necessary to name every single dish, but who's to tell her?

He read out the numbers next to the dishes, loudly and clearly. No need to give the waiter the satisfaction of hearing him mangle the fancy names.

"Number twenty-six, twenty-eight, and forty-five it'll be sir," the waiter repeated with an asinine giggle. His pencil hung from a velvet cord around his neck.

"How about an apéritif, sir? For the lady perhaps. This week we are featuring several Valentine's Day specials. I highly recommend Love on the Beach." The waiter smiled fondly at Shanti.

Shanti glanced quickly at Anand's bent head and shook her head jerkily, embarrassed.

Valentine's Day! Since when did they have that in India? Utter crap!

"Just get us the food, will you?" Vishnukumar snapped, and the waiter buzzed off, his smile still in place. The idiot was probably trained in this kind of thing. Lesson 1: How to Make the Poor Middle Class Sod Who Wanders into Our Super High Class Restaurant Feel Out of Place.

Anand looked up from his electronic game. "Today the principal called a special assembly about Valentine's Day," the boy announced. "Some big boys are sending some girls cards so they banned it. They asked Sreeja and Kalpana who got the cards to stand up in front of the whole school. Adil and I saw them crying near the bathrooms afterward—"

"Valentine's Day! Your principal's absolutely right. Whoever heard of such rubbish!" Vishnukumar interrupted.

"Shhh . . . let the boy finish," Shanti said. "Are they sending cards already? I thought Valentine's Day was the day after to-morrow." She reached over and straightened Anand's collar. "Did any of your friends send cards?"

Anand smiled and looked down at his game. Was he blushing? He was eleven for God's sake. Too early for this kind of thing. Anand, hope you haven't started already.

Vishnukumar opened his mouth and closed it. Best not to say anything—after all this was supposed to be a special occasion for the boy. His first time out with them on their anniversary. Shanti had insisted. A reward for turning eleven, she'd said. He'd reminded Shanti that when *he* turned eleven all his dad had done was increase his weekly allowance to the princely sum of two rupees, but she wouldn't listen. She spoiled the boy too much. This is what came with having just one kid. No! He wouldn't think of all that now.

"I hope the Mothers eat dinner—I put everything on the table," Shanti said very softly, so Anand wouldn't hear. So that was the problem. She was worrying about the *after* as usual.

"Forget it. We eat in a restaurant once a year, for God's sake." Every year it was the same damn thing. If it wasn't the Mothers it was something else. She didn't know how to relax anymore.

"Grandmother told me that she didn't feel like having dinner since she'd have to eat alone," Mr. Little Pitcher with Big Ears Anand reported. Shanti looked anxious. The sharp vertical lines between her eyebrows framed the red dot of her bindi, as if to keep it in place. He quickly pointed out the ice cream choices on the menu to Anand to distract him.

The Mothers had each other—they weren't alone. Although the two old ladies hadn't eaten together for years, technically they were not alone in the house. Of course, most of the time they acted as if they hated each other, although his mother had eased off on the sniping a bit since Shanti's mother had started showing signs of Alzheimer's. Funny how he thought of it like that—Alzheimer's—as if it was some innocuous surname like Patel or Rao.

The food arrived at last in polished copper urns, each dish kept warm by the bright blue flame of its personal brazier. Anand was vociferous in his appreciation and the waiter returned to the kitchen smirking, deeply gratified no doubt.

"I am glad that we do this only once a year—this is too damn expensive. As if the food at Moti Mahal isn't good enough," he said. Although the food wasn't bad. Number twenty-six, or was it forty-five, was a standout, the shrimp curry sharp with tamarind and fennel.

"Don't start your Gandhism now please," Shanti hissed just as he opened his mouth to commend the food.

There she goes again. She had to bring up that silly term here too. Everything was blamed on his Gandhism. His refusal to buy a scooter. His dislike of shoes. His preference for kurta pyjamas. No use explaining that millions of people traveled by bus to work every day. Or that when it was so goddamn hot it made sense to wear cotton clothes. Every so often nowadays he heard, It's not as if we are poor—you are Dr. Vishnukumar, B.A., M.A., Ph.D., Mister Big Shot Assistant Editor, and you go to the office in sandals like an ordinary peon and make your wife hang by a strap in a crowded bus. Nyaah nyaah nyaah. He particularly hated the way she dragged out his degrees. Still, her arthritis was getting worse. Arthritis at forty-four, who'd ever heard of such a thing? But who's to tell her that the thought of weaving through the teeming streets on a scooter made him feel nauseated.

He took a deep breath, then another. Anyway, best not to spoil the dinner with you said this and I said that. Best to shut up and eat chicken à la coriander or whatever the hell this was and order ice cream and keep everything all silky smiley smooth and hope like hell it stayed that way once they got home.

She didn't want to do it. That too on their anniversary! They always did it on their anniversary. I am fed up, she said. Turned her back on him and said this is the last anniversary we go out, it's not the same anymore. He lay flat on his back and watched the blades of the fan slash at the faint blue light that seeped up from the street. Granted the Mothers had done everything they could to mess things up from the moment the three of them had stepped through the door. In his irrepressible enthusiasm Anand had blurted out, We had three-color ice cream, and there had been dead silence from the end of the room. The Mothers had stared at him fishy-eyed as if eating ice cream was equal to murder. Squashed the boy's good mood with immediate effect. Then Shanti's mother had noticed that someone had left the front door open and rolled her wheelchair forward like a demented race car driver.

"Can I close the door? Shouldn't the door be closed? Will someone please close the door? Anand, close the door. Lock it lock it lock it," she'd screamed.

Then, once the door was locked, she started on the windows. They had to be shut too—although it was bloody one hundred degrees outside. No use telling her they were safe inside the house. She'd forget right away. Her memory was a wave, barely touching the shores of the moment before it receded again.

"There are eyes, watching . . . ," she'd said, peering at the dark outside. They had tried ignoring her before. Then she'd slap her hand across her forehead, pound her fist against her own chest. Doing what she wanted was easier. He had shut all the windows, drawn the curtains over the dark panes himself, held the curtains up to show her the fastened latches, and talked to her quietly until she had registered that they were closed. To top it all, to take the bloody cake, she hadn't eaten her dinner. Typical, really.

"Always this eating, eating . . . Who cares about food?" she'd said when Shanti asked her. "*She* ate . . . I saw her," she'd said and nodded accusingly at his mother, who just sat there rolling her last chew for the night, not saying a word at all the drama.

His mother had ignored the old lady, but had looked at

Shanti sharply. "Is that another new sari?" she'd mumbled through her fingers, packing the tobacco into the corners of her mouth.

Shanti hadn't answered but she'd banged the bedroom door a bit too loudly. He shifted in the bed and Shanti sighed in her sleep. Shanti had changed these days. He was always being surprised by some sharp bit of her that suddenly stuck out and poked at him. Maybe her time was coming—the whole female change thing. Maybe the no-go tonight was for the best, what with both the old ladies all agitated. Probably lying wide awake right now on the opposite side of the door, both of them in their separate beds.

Although Shanti and he were the world's greatest experts at doing it on the quiet. They'd done it in silence for years—ever since the Mothers had moved in. Correction. One Mother. His. In the beginning there was one. You didn't exactly moan and shout in ecstasy when only a thick curtain separated you from your only living parent. Not that he could blame Mother.

He hadn't been able to afford anything better in those days—when was it? A year, maybe six months after they were married. Shanti hadn't said too much about Mother living with them. She was like that, kept everything deep inside, away from anyone's reach. There had been that whole business when she stopped eating for a week, but she had come around. She'd understood that a man had obligations and duties. One did what one had to do, he'd always been clear about that. When your father died you looked after your mother. Right? Right! And he, Vishnukumar, B.A., M.A., Ph.D., always obeyed the rules.

Although it had worked out all right. His mother had taken over the cooking. And she'd taken care of Anand. If Shanti were honest she'd admit that her promotions at the college had come faster because she hadn't taken a year off after her delivery like all the other teachers. Not that she saw it like that. What was it she'd said a few years ago? I live like a guest here, or something cryptic like that. He had thought about that sentence for days, imagined elaborate scenarios where he explained his position on these matters to her. But then there were things you did and things you didn't. And you didn't talk about your mother with your wife. Or vice versa.

"Shut up! It's only seven o'clock, you crazy bird!" The damned bird outside the window was repeating the same note over and over, sounding delirious. It was too early in the morning for that kind of thing. He liked to drink his coffee and brood over the headlines in the rival papers. Make mental notes on which subeditor needed to be pulled up for missing some important local news. But the bird was disturbing the peace. And uh-oh here was Mother. His mother sidled up to him. Now see here, morning is my time, damn it, so go away. Women! He'd had it up to here with them. Nyaah nyaah nyaah—that was their sound of choice. Wouldn't leave him alone—even so early in the morning.

Conversation between him and Mother had been restricted, to say the least, in recent years. She'd turned quieter, as if old age had slowed her voice down to a trickle. Mornings are off limits, Mother. He put aside the paper and waited without saying a word. Usually she delivered one precise sentence and left. Okay, so let's have it, Mother, and this time try and stretch the copy to at least fifty words.

"There is hardly enough rice left for tomorrow and my tobacco's almost gone," she said.

He nodded and turned back to the paper. Vishnukumar,

make mental note. Item one: Rice. Item two: Tobacco. Okay. Shall do. Will deliver. Back to the foreign pages. Some idiot misspelled Herzegovina and no one noticed. No, wait, there's more to come. She stood there until he looked up at her. There was a glittering fervor in her eyes. What, he said.

"Shanti's doing it again," she said. "Thinks she can hide it from me but I know—two new saris, one salwar kameez. Hidden on the top shelf of the cupboard. Behind the bedsheets. I've seen them. I know." She nodded her head, satisfied with her vigilance.

Gawd. Here it was again, the old spying game. Mother should have worked at the paper. She'd have gone after every story like a mongoose after a snake. His mother had always reported all Shanti's purchases to him as if it were her duty. Not that he cared—you didn't have to be Hercule Poirot and sport a mustache to realize that Shanti hid her shopping from his mother. But invariably she'd ferret out Shanti's secret stash like an eager bloodhound.

He knew what to say, had said the same thing for years.

"I'll tell her," he said, before the old lady could say anything else, and ducked back into the paper. As if. He'd never ask Shanti to stop hiding her purchases. Although the woman did spend too much. How many saris did she need? He'd never ask his mother to give up her relentless pursuit of Shanti either. This had nothing to do with him; their contest had been going on for years.

The boy was babbling at the dining table. Something about Valentine's Day again. It seemed to be in the headlines around this house a lot lately. He'd never seen Anand so excited about events at school. Except for the time he wrote that long essay about monsoon patterns over the last decade in South India and the teacher punished him. He'd done a lot of research too, on the Internet. The teacher had asked them to write about "My Favorite Season," or something dead boring like that. Ha. Anand had been younger and so outraged at being pulled up in front of all the others in class. Ha ha. He had been so pleased with the way the boy was shaping up that he'd gone out and bought him all eight volumes of Edward Gibbon's *Decline and Fall of the Roman Empire* as a birthday present, not caring that it cost an astonishing 1,700 rupees. And now all the boy did was sit open-mouthed in front of the TV. He should have stuck to his guns and never succumbed to their nagging for the box. Millions lived without it.

"Today they found out that the girls were also sending cards to the boys. The principal said many bad things to them. He said they had no—" Anand stopped and got up from the table, took a piece of paper out of his book bag, and read the word out loud "—'Propriety.' What does that mean?"

"Never mind. Your principal is wrong in making a big fuss about all this," Shanti said.

"No. The principal's right. It's a racket—it's just bloody TV and all these American card companies wanting to make money. They even have Secretaries Day nowadays. Say the words to your secretary—as the ad says on TV. Imagine. Secretary Sues Boss over Card. Alleges Improper Conduct."

"What's 'alleges'?" Anand asked.

"Nothing. Anand, you are not to watch cable except for Discovery and National Geographic," he said.

"Every single thing is not some imperialist plot to destroy India's glorious traditions," Shanti said. "I think Valentine's Day is good."

Good. What kind of argument was that? Good was nothing. It was ice on a hot frying pan. And sarcasm, my girl, will get you nowhere. Why did she care anyway? As if she'd grown up sending cards or whatever the hell else people did on Valentine's bloody Day.

The two of them were on their usual after-dinner amble around the park when she brought it up again. Positively bristling. The school was awful, so backward, it was wrong to punish the children for showing their feelings, after all it was only an expression of affection, affection had to be shown once in a while, didn't it? What was wrong with that? Why did these people have to stifle natural impulses, and so on and so forth. What was she so excited about?

When he tuned back in, she was talking about some Vimla.

"Who's Vimla?" he said.

"The adjunct for First Year English. I've told you about her. Anyway, she said her husband has booked a table for February 14."

His library books were overdue, he remembered suddenly. Maybe he could drop them off on his way to work tomorrow.

". . . so that's why they've decided to celebrate Valentine's Day," Shanti said.

"Who?" he asked, confused.

"Vimla and her husband. I just told you."

Was she still talking about Valentine's Day? She had this tendency to repeat things. Perhaps it ran in the family. Like mother like daughter. Yesterday her mother had stopped him as he was leaving for work and asked him where her parents were. He had explained that they were dead, she was seventy-five and so her parents had to have grown old and died, hadn't they? She had started wailing. He had quietly held her hands until she'd noticed the open window and asked him to close it with the tears still running down her face. She'd asked him the same questions about her parents two days ago. And sobbed then too. Her mourning was always new, just as painful and as fleeting every time.

If one could manage to go without getting older, to vanish at night quietly in one's sleep, that would be a true blessing. Gandhi had died in one true shot, a bullet that abruptly interceded between one breath and the next.

"Mother is getting worse, isn't she?" Shanti asked. He said nothing. What was there to say? Yes, she's worse and it'll be awful soon, but there's nothing to do except go through with it.

He didn't know what else one could do, really. Shanti's brother, Mr. Multinational Managing Director, had made noises about the new old age homes that were springing up all over— "better care," he'd mumbled over the phone. Not that Big Shot himself was willing to have anything to do with the old lady— used to send her back to Shanti before his allotted three months of mother-care rotation were up. The man's own mother! Always had the excuses ready too—children couldn't bring their friends home, she didn't get along with his wife—until Vishnukumar finally said enough and refused to send the old lady to Shanti's brother's place anymore. Of course, his own mother had started going on about tradition and the old what-will-people-say, how can you have your wife's mother hanging around your house, you are the son-in-law and you should act like it, and all that kind of nonsense, until he had to tell her to shut up. Mother still hadn't forgiven him that particular episode. It had been a bit tough at first with the two old ladies arguing and nagging Anand and Shanti—but he'd told everyone that there was no way out. This was the way it was.

"I'm losing hair," Shanti said. "Look." She was pointing to a patch on her head. The scalp did show through, pale pink under the street lamp. It was shocking, as if he had seen some secret, uncharted part of her.

"We'll see a doctor, a skin specialist." She combed her hair over the bare spot, he realized suddenly. That's why he hadn't noticed.

"What's the point? It's my mother. Her scenes. I get so . . . so . . ." She stopped, her eyes filling with tears.

"We'll see a skin specialist. Dr. Kumar is good—remember when Anand got that rash? He'll know what to do." He patted her hair, smoothed it down, tucked a few strands behind her ears. She had had beautiful thick hair until the arthritis set in. He'd wind it around his throat and pretend to choke to death. Once upon a time.

He gave her arm a slight squeeze. She was so much thinner these days. He searched for his handkerchief so she could wipe her eyes, but couldn't find it.

"We'll go on Friday. I'll call the doctor from work." What else was there to say? He was never very good at the sappy stuff: the arm around the shoulder and all that. Anyway, they were outside with all the nosy neighbors hanging onto their gates, waiting for exactly such aberrations to gossip about.

So: back to base. Home sweet home. Shanti went off to bed early, leaving him alone to read his book. Everyone else was mercifully asleep—the boy curled up like a shrimp when he went to look in on him. He opened his book and sat with it in his lap. *The Castle.* To think that Kafka had been a mere insurance clerk most of his life. Just goes to show that it wasn't necessary to travel the world to be creative, to experience life. Gandhi had come back from South Africa and stayed put, but created a revolution anyway. He'd mentioned Kafka to Shanti when she brought up the fact that all the junior editors had snagged high-class jobs in Singapore and Dubai. Well, at least Kafka wrote books, she'd said.

Shanti had changed. Gotten jagged and uneven. All this buying all the time. Sari after sari. He'd decided it wasn't worth saying anything. She always got an excited look on her face when she showed them off to him. They closed the door from his mother and whispered together like conspirators. When their parents had arranged their marriage she had written him letters and he had replied. All their conversation had been words on paper. News clippings of life in the city and poems he had secretly written in between obituaries, astrology columns, and the rest of the drudgery of early journalism. Those days there had been no phone in her house where he could call and ask to hear her voice. Even after they were married she had continued being the quiet one. First with shyness, and then Mother had arrived. Shanti had just fallen into the habit of saying little. But nowadays she was different—going on about something or other, as if the years had stuffed words into her until they overflowed. Age gets you in the end, changes you into something you wouldn't have imagined, someone you would have recoiled from when you were younger.

Long ago, a few years after his mother had come to stay, he had taken Shanti along to the Conference of Regional Newspapers and they had stayed in a hotel room in Mysore. He had shown her the phone numbers for room service and picked up the phone to pretend-order plates of butter chicken and lamb biryani for breakfast. He'd come out of the bathroom and been surprised to see two steaming cups of coffee on the table and her giggling in the corner. She had ordered room service on her own for the first time in her life. They drank their coffee on the balcony, she still in her flowered nightie, sunlight caught in the hollows of her collarbones, and he'd made up silly stuff about the men who floated in the pool, potbellies up. They were just two anonymous people in a hotel full of strangers and he had groaned out loud in his pleasure that night, but she hadn't made a sound—it had already been too late. By then the habit of silence had gone too deep.

The phone rang. It was the new stringer from Pune calling

at this time of the night just so he could wake everyone in the house. There were mistakes in the story he had filed yesterday, he wheezed, the paper'll have to publish an addendum or errata, so sorry about the oversight. That's what came of hiring these inexperienced puppies. He'd tried telling them a million times but the jackass editor waffled on about austerity measures. As if anyone with half a brain didn't know that the term was only bullshit legalese for we-are-too-cheap-to-pay-real-reporters.

He knelt down to look at yesterday's edition of the paper, riffling through the mess of newspapers thrown under the sofa. He turned the pages to the national briefs searching for the story, but someone had scissored out half the stringer's report along with other parts of the paper, leaving see-through holes surrounded by the spider scrawl of yesterday's news. All the way from the second page to the last. Goddamnit!

He went into Anand's bedroom. Had to shake him awake and ask him if he had mutilated the paper for some worthless school project. The boy started bawling and carrying on like a baby and Vishnukumar had to hold him and run his fingers through his hair until he went back to sleep. Right! So if it wasn't Anand, then who was it? The Mothers? Not bloody likely. They usually liked to destroy whole pages, wrap prayer books with the colorful Sunday sections, but they wouldn't cut stuff out. He had to find that missing article and phone in the corrections or get dressed right now and go to the office. It was too damn much. Why hadn't the idiot stringer just called the night desk?

"What's the matter with you, why are you wandering about waking everyone in the middle of the night?" Shanti asked from the doorway.

Great! Just perfect. That's all he needed, her awake and

grouching. "Go to sleep. Someone in this house cut up the paper and the boy denies everything. He's learning to lie in his sleep," he whispered loudly.

She stood there looking at him for minutes, and her face twisted strangely. "You need that right now? Those missing bits . . ."

She spoke as if she hadn't heard him. Arrggh! This was serious. He had no time to stand there listening to her waffle on. "I'll have to go to the office now—I can't phone in the corrections without the lines in front of me, can I? The article on unknown page about literacy among women in Maharashtra, misstated on line so-and-so the number of women illiterates as such-and-such when it should actually have been 64,000." He couldn't quite get away with that now, could he? The chief sub would think he was drunk, making him hunt around for one article out of a hundred in yesterday's edition.

"So you do need it now," Shanti said.

Ah ha! Enlightenment at last. She was standing there, looking as if someone had stolen her jewelry.

"Go back to sleep, this is my problem," he said.

She motioned him into the bedroom. "Look behind the bedsheets. On the top shelf," she said, opening the cupboard.

He didn't have the time to look at her latest purchases, this was a bloody crisis, in case she hadn't noticed.

"I'll have to get a chair to reach up there. Why don't you just do it?" she said.

Gawd. All right, all right. He stood on his toes, reached into the back of the shelf behind the bedsheets, and pulled out the neat squares of newsprint lying on top of her hoard of new clothes. He flipped through them quickly, found the stringer's story on women's literacy, and phoned the office with the corrections.

As the subeditor on the other end wrote it down he turned over the cutouts idly and read the ads on the other side. Romantic Candlelit Dinner with Live Music Only Rs. 500, Rediscover the Girl You Married (Free Bottle Of Wine with Rs. 650 Option). So many ads, all cut out so precisely. The prices were shocking for dinner for just two people. Obviously the restaurants were making a packet out of this whole Valentine's Day frenzy. But the silly people who rushed off dutifully like morons to do the TV's bidding deserved to be robbed. That would make a good editorial; he could link it up with other ways America got the country to spend money . . . the IMF's many demands and all that kind of thing. When he went back into the bedroom, he thought of waking Shanti to tell her about it. He was pretty sure she was awake anyway, something about the way she was lying there, but then suddenly he didn't feel like talking . . . Begin by composing a brilliant editorial opening sentence, Vishnukumar . . .

Shanti had cut out the ads and hidden them behind the bedsheets with her saris. She had been bringing up the whole Valentine's Day thing again and again and now she had cut out the ads. And hidden them. Even from him. His mother had always pointed out her silly subterfuges and he hadn't cared. Hadn't ever brought it up with her either. He didn't blame her. She had put up with a lot. The Mothers for one. Her arthritis that had come on just days after the baby had died. She had carried her around inside her for two days after she had stopped moving, not knowing, not noticing that she was no longer kicking fourteen days into the eighth month. He had thought about the baby on their anniversary at the Municipal Aquarium, where they had gone, the three of them, one more treat for Anand's eleventh. He'd always enjoyed the aquarium, almost as much as the boy did. There was something mesmerizing about the big fish moving ponderously through the water, their slick heads and silently moving mouths always questing for food.

Anand had pressed his face onto the glass and said it was cool how everything blurred and looked different and so Vishnukumar had done the same on the other side of the glass for fun. He'd seen the boy's face and his wet flattened lips distorted by the bubbled water, his head almost adrift in the shadows of the tank, the fish floating slowly past in the fluid, and the tears had begun. He had stood there for a long time, his face pressed against the cool glass, and had felt sick and tired and scared of everything that had gone before and that was still to come. Then he had wiped his eyes with the cotton hanky Shanti ironed and put into his pocket every morning, collected her, pried the boy away from the glass, wiped away some more tears quickly while mother and son were busy crossing the street, and herded them all into the restaurant. And had made fun of the waiter's earring until he could breathe properly again.

He could still do it all, could still manage to keep them all running in place, somehow. Eh, Vishnukumar? You can still do it, can't you?

Almost dawn. He heard the morning paper land with a thud outside. One more paper to cut ads out of, eh girl? Stupid bastard stringer and his fucking errata. Fucked up the whole stupid night. These goddamn incompetents he was forced to work with made him want to puke all over their shiny patent leather shoes. And it was so fucking cold in here in the early morning but of course he could never turn off the bloody fan because Shanti's arthritis medicine made her hot all the time. Every day it was the same stupid bloody thing. All the sickening admin work. Chase this sub, call that stringer, write another fucking middle-of-the-road edit. But then he knew all about that, didn't he, Vishnukumar? Middle-of-the-roadness. Stay-on-their-good-sideness. He was the fucking principal of the don't rock the boat do your job and take the money and go home school of thinking. It was what one did, just one more goddamn stupid fucking thing that one had to do and did. All of one's life, day after day after fucking day.

When he left the house to go to the office the next morning it was Valentine's Day, and the street had gone crazy. He stood outside the gate for minutes, not moving. There were balloons. Shiny heart-shaped balloons floating above the sidewalk, plump and obscene. Balloons bobbing officiously in front of shops. Streamers shimmering in the morning light, their pink letters screaming LOVE. The neighborhood looked so different, it was goddamn unnerving. The world had changed overnight. He set off across the park toward the bus stop. There was a crowd of teenagers, the girls in white school uniforms, the boys wearing suits and ties, some no older than Anand, milling about in the park. A few had the same vulgar red balloons straining and wobbling in the breeze, tethered to their hot little hands. Others had huge bunches of yellow roses, blowsy and overblown already although it was still early in the morning. He hesitated as he neared the kids, then decided it couldn't be helped. He just wouldn't buy their silly roses, that's all.

They must have seen him vacillate on the path because they surrounded him in minutes, yelling Happy Valentine's Day. He smiled and made to move on, but they wouldn't let him. Uncle, please buy a balloon, please buy a flower for your wife, Uncle, they yelled in his ear. Then they started waving roses under his nose. He sneezed and they laughed like hyenas. For God's sake. Didn't these kids have anything better to do so early in the morning? This was getting ridiculous. Let me through, he said, and batted at one plump girl's hand, perhaps a little too roughly. That was enough to set them off. Let Uncle through, let Uncle through, they chanted and crowded in closer. They laughed and shouted and pushed each other onto him. The fat girl whose hand he had hit, her cheeks quivering, almost pulled his arm out of its socket and yelled Happy Valentine's Day so close to his face that he could see the strands of spittle in her throat. Her bunch of flowers hit him on the chin. It's only five rupees for one, show love, Uncle, buy one and show love, she screamed. Go on, buy one, the proceeds go to charity, one of the bigger boys said, practically shoving his grimy palm into his middle. Buy a rose, buy a rose, they chanted in unison and jostled him roughly, pushing him into the center of their tight little circle, grabbing at the strap of his cloth bag that swung wildly from his shoulders. They are only being boisterous, they are kids just playing, calm down Vishnukumar, try breathing slower. His heart was galloping in his chest. Then one tall boy tried to trip him and suddenly he was struggling and yelling for the police like a madman, the panic setting in, tearing at the press of hot bodies, lashing out at their roses and balloons.

He broke through the circle and ran. A few of the buggers ran after him jeering and cat-calling, even bunged a small stone that hurtled past his ear. But he kept running and after some time they stopped following him. All right, Vishnukumar, away from the main road and into this side street now. Safe. You are safe here. He felt faint, could feel the thin cotton of his kurta sticking to his skin. Safe. He sat down on the curb next to an overflowing trash can. Bloody municipality, everything's a mess in this country. He'd just sit here quietly for a few minutes and find another, roundabout way to the bus stop when his breathing got better. Deep breaths now. In. Hold. Out. In. Hold. Out. He found his hanky and wiped his face and then buried his face in his knees. When he looked up there was another group of children, bristling with balloons and roses, gathering at the corner, a procession of potential tormentors about to turn into the street. There was even a fat girl leading the pack, only this time she was wearing a green-and-white-checked uniform. They hadn't seen him yet. Up, up, and away, Vishnukumar. Round the big concrete trash can now. A god-awful stink but big enough to hide him. He ducked down behind the trash can and knelt there. As the revelers streamed past, he made sure he didn't peer out even once. Finally their shouts grew fainter and the street returned to its morning quietness. He got up stiffly from his crouch and stepped into the street looking up and down its length, hoping it was safe to go on his way and that the danger was truly past.

The fat girl in the checked uniform was coming down the street. Must have fallen behind the others. She was shuffling along quietly, the last few roses hanging limply from her fingers. He jerked back onto the sidewalk and she smiled at him. Head down, Vishnukumar, straight march ahead. If she came near him he'd ignore her.

"Uncle, how about a rose?" she asked.

"No, no rose," he said quickly. Keep walking, keep walking. She stepped in front of him holding the flowers up to him.

"I got them from our garden. I thought I'd sell them all." The kid wouldn't leave him alone. "Please. There are only a few left," she whined. In the slanted light of the early morning the roses were pale yellow, their waxy petals still tightly furled.

Okay, okay. Anything to get out of here. He pulled out his purse, found the money, and took the flowers from the girl. She grinned at him like a fool and practically skipped down the road. He was sure he looked damn silly standing there with the roses in his hand. How the hell was he supposed to manage these flowers? Goddamn nuisance really. He laid them horizontally in the bottom of his bag and zipped up its edges so the roses wouldn't show. The trick was to keep them safe until he got back to the house. Shanti would know what to do with them. She'd find a vase or something. He imagined her face when she opened the door and saw him with the flowers. He'd hand them to her and leave quickly, no waiting around for the question and answer session, he decided. Then he turned and started up the road toward home.

Acknowledgments

I am grateful to my father for introducing me to the delights of language and to my mother for her unwavering enthusiasm. I am indebted to Melissa Hammerle for creating a nurturing and productive environment at NYU's Creative Writing Program. I am grateful to E. L. Doctorow for his helpful advice on my thesis. The wise counsel and generosity of Breyten Breytenbach has been invaluable. My teachers Chuck Wachtel, Irini Spanidou, Toby Olson, Alan Singer, and Joan Mellen have enriched my writing immeasurably. I thank the *New York Times* Company Foundation for their support. Thanks are also due to the following people: Josh Marston and Raj Parameswaran for their insights and honesty; Siobhan Broderick, friend and sounding board; Jessica Weetch and Dave Purcell, fellow travelers; Ailish Ryan, for her everwilling ear; LuAnn Walther, my perceptive and patient editor; and my agent, Ellen Levine, for her commitment and hard work. Finally I thank Arun, without whom nothing is possible.